TWO-TIME LOSER

Grifter lunged, his huge arms outstretched, sadistic glee curling his lips. He thought he had Fargo dead to rights. He was dead wrong.

Shifting, the Trailsman rammed his rifle barrel into Grifter's gut. Grifter doubled over, flushing scarlet. Clutching his abdomen, he tottered, spittle flecking his chin.

"How about you two?" Fargo asked Grifter's surviving sidekicks. Both vigorously shook their heads.

But Grifter did not know when he was well off. He snarled, "No one does that to me! No one! By the time I'm through, you'll beg me to put you out of your misery, you son of a—"

He got no further. Fargo swung the Henry in a tight arc, the stock catching Grifter squarely on the cheek and splitting it like an overripe melon. Grifter staggered, blood spurting. A roar of rage spewed from his throat, and he lunged again. Fargo brought the stock up and around, smashing it against Grifter's jaw. Teeth crunched. Like melting wax, the giant bruiser oozed to the earth, unconscious.

Fargo looked down at him and smiled thinly. Double the trouble, double the fun . . . and Skye had a hunch the fun was just starting. . . .

BE SURE TO READ THE OTHER THRILLING NOVELS IN THE EXCITING *TRAILSMAN* SERIES!

⦿ SIGNET

TRAILSMAN SERIES BY JON SHARPE

THE
TRAILSMAN
#190

PECOS
DEATH

by

Jon Sharpe

A SIGNET BOOK

SIGNET
Published by the Penguin Group
Penguin Putnam Inc., 375 Hudson Street,
New York, New York 10014, U.S.A.
Penguin Books Ltd, 27 Wrights Lane,
London W8 5TZ, England
Penguin Books Australia Ltd,
Ringwood, Victoria, Australia
Penguin Books Canada Ltd, 10 Alcorn Avenue,
Toronto, Ontario, Canada M4V 3B2
Penguin Books (N.Z.) Ltd, 182-190 Wairau Road,
Auckland 10, New Zealand

Penguin Books Ltd, Registered Offices:
Harmondsworth, Middlesex, England

First published by Signet, an imprint of Dutton Signet,
a member of Penguin Putnam Inc.

First Printing, October, 1997
10 9 8 7 6 5 4 3 2 1

The first chapter of this book originally appeared in *Missouri Massacre*,
the one hundred eighty-ninth volume in this series.

 REGISTERED TRADEMARK—MARCA REGISTRADA

Printed in the United States of America

The Trailsman

Beginnings . . . they bend the tree and they mark the man. Skye Fargo was born when he was eighteen. Terror was his midwife, vengeance his first cry. Killing spawned Skye Fargo, ruthless, cold-blooded murder. Out of the acrid smoke of gunpowder still hanging in the air, he rose, cried out a promise never forgotten.

The Trailsman they began to call him all across the West: searcher, scout, hunter, the man who could see where others only looked, his skills for hire but not his soul, the man who lived each day to the fullest, yet trailed each tomorrow. Skye Fargo, the Trailsman, and the seeker who could take the wildness of a land and the wanting of a woman and make them his own.

1860—New Mexico Territory,
where coyotes skulk on two legs
and hatreds threaten to spark a wildfire . . .

1

Gunshots blasted crisp and clear in the dry New Mexico air. Five loud ones in swift succession, followed by two more, fainter. Skye Fargo had no trouble pinpointing the direction they came from. Hardly had the sounds faded than the big man tapped his spurs against the Ovaro and galloped toward a rise to the south.

The Trailsman was in hostile country, on temporary dispatch duty for the army. There were Apaches to watch out for. Utes, as well. Not to mention roving bands of cutthroats who preyed in growing numbers on unwary travelers, renegades and outcasts who had given New Mexico a reputation for not being fit for greenhorns.

Not that anyone would ever brand Skye Fargo a tenderfoot. Tall, broad-shouldered, and powerfully built, he was the sort of man others tended to shy from. One look into his piercing lake blue eyes was enough to convince most people that riling him would have the same result as riling a grizzly.

Hat brim pulled low against the blistering sun, Fargo reined up just below the crest. Rising in the stirrups, he scanned the arid terrain beyond.

New Mexico in July was an oven. Shimmering waves of heat rippled from the baked earth. Mesquite, yucca, and purple sage grew where little else could, the sage adding a dash of color to the otherwise bleak landscape. Of wildlife there was no sign, with the lone exception of a large hawk lazily circling.

Fargo ventured higher, taking the risk of exposing himself in the hope of locating the source of the gunfire. Almost immediately, from a canyon on his right echoed another ragged volley. It was answered by two single shots spaced seconds apart. From the sound of things, someone with a pistol was up against three or four rifles.

Few lone riders would bother to investigate. It was simply too risky a proposition. On the frontier, any *hombre* who stuck his nose in where it did not belong ran the risk of having his fool head shot off. For all Fargo knew, Apaches were involved, and no one in his right mind cared to tangle with the Mescaleros or Jicarillas.

Yet Fargo did not hesitate. Someone might need help, and he was the only help handy. Flicking his reins, he trotted to the canyon mouth. Along the way he slid his shiny Henry rifle from its scabbard. Working the lever, he fed a .44 cartridge into the chamber.

Ground chewed up by hoofprints told part of the story. A lone rider had been chased into the canyon by four others. Who they were, and what they were doing so far from civilization was a mystery Fargo aimed to solve by dismounting and warily catfooting forward.

Rifles thundered, the retorts rumbling off the high stone walls like so much thunder. Somewhere a horse whinnied in pain. The pistol answered the rifles, only to be drowned out by another blistering round of leaden fury.

Around the next bend the clash raged. Fargo crept to the edge, then peeked out. Acrid smoke hung thick and heavy, wafting above a large boulder that shielded four riflemen. Their backs were to him. Two were armed with Henrys, one with a Sharps, the last held a Volcanic Arms carbine.

A grungy character whose red bandanna was stained with grime motioned for the others to stop firing. Cupping a hand to his mouth, he hollered, "Cambridge, this is Grifter! Make it easy on yourself! Toss those saddlebags out where we can get 'em, and we'll take 'em and skedaddle. What do you say?"

No one answered.

"Use your head, damn it!" the grimy man said. "Is it worth your life? You don't owe Stockwell anything."

Still, Cambridge did not respond.

"I'm tryin' to be reasonable," Grifter huffed. "But if this is how you want it, fine by me. We can wait you out, you know. We have plenty of water. But you can't get to your canteen without us blowin' your head off." He paused to let that bit of information sink in. "So what will it be? Do you hand it over or not?"

Cambridge answered with a shot that whined off the boulder. Flying rock slivers forced Grifter and his friends to duck. Swearing luridly, Grifter gave the order to fire and all four men cut loose, their rifles hammering in deafening cadence. They only stopped when they emptied their weapons.

Fargo had no idea what the fight was about, or who was in the right. But he had taken an instinctive dislike to Grifter. The man was a human sidewinder if ever there was one. And Grifter's companions were cut from the same coarse cloth. He was about to show himself when a strident nicker reminded him of the stricken horse.

A weasel in baggy pants and a floppy hat moved to the end of the boulder, fed a cartridge into his Sharps, and took deliberate aim. "I hate for any critter to suffer," he commented.

Grifter chortled. "Let the nag raise a fuss, Zeke. Maybe it'll convince that stubborn yack to do what's best."

"It ain't right to let anything die slow and painful," Zeke insisted. "My pa taught me that when I was still a sprout."

"Lordy!" Grifter said, nudging one of the others. "Hear that, Hardwick? We got us a Good Samaritan here! Next

11

thing you know, he'll climb up on this boulder and give us a sermon about how we have to mend our wicked ways."

Hardwick and the fourth man snickered. Zeke shifted from one foot to the other and said sullenly, "I won't do no such thing, neither. All I'm sayin' is—"

"I know what you're sayin'!" Grifter unexpectedly exploded, lunging and seizing Zeke by the front of his homespun shirt. "The problem is that you're talkin' when you should be listenin'! I want the stinkin' horse left to rot. You got that?"

Zeke had blanched. Swallowing hard, he bobbed his pointed chin. "Sure, Tom. Sure. Don't get yourself in a huff. I know better than to buck you."

"You'd better," Grifter said, shoving the smaller man against the boulder. "I don't like being sassed. Ever."

The man called Hardwick fished cartridges from a shirt pocket. Bearded and unkempt, he had a belly that would do justice to a hog. "Do you really aim to sit here in this hot sun and wait Cambridge out?"

"A little sweat won't kill you," Grifter said. "As soon as it's dark, the four of us will close in. We should be able to sneak right up on her."

Fargo stiffened. Had he heard correctly? *Her?* Leveling the Henry, he inched around the corner. The four men were so busy reloading that they had no inkling of his presence. Less than ten feet from them, he planted both boots and declared, "Drop the rifles, gents."

All four spun. Hardwick and the fourth man froze. Zeke's mouth worked like that of a carp out of water, his eyelids fluttering like butterfly wings. Grifter started to bring up his rifle, stopping only when the muzzle of Fargo's Henry swung toward his stomach.

"Didn't you hear me? Set the hardware down, boys. Real slow."

Reluctantly, baffled anger contorting his features, Grifter

complied. It was the cue for the others to do likewise. Zeke promptly elevated his hands. Hardwick, though, held his left arm cocked as if he were tempted to make a stab for his Remington revolver.

"If you reckon you're faster than a bullet, go ahead," Fargo said, smirking. "If not, I'd advise all of you to shuck the belt guns."

Livid with fury, Grifter unbuckled his gunbelt and lowered it to the ground. "I don't like it when others butt into my affairs," he growled.

Fargo was watching Hardwick. The heavyset cutthroat was taking his sweet time unbuckling. He wasn't fooling anyone. Hardwick was itching to turn the tables and was hoping Fargo would lower his guard for just a second.

"What's your stake in this, mister?" Grifter asked, eyes glittering like those of a rabid wolf eager to pounce. "Who the hell are you, anyway?"

Ignoring him, Fargo angled toward them. He gazed deeper into the canyon as if trying to spot the person they had been shooting at. Out of the corner of his eye he saw Hardwick begin to ease the gunbelt down. The gunman was holding it in such a way that the holster was close to his stomach, and close to his right hand.

Suddenly Hardwick clawed at the Remington. He was fast, all right, but not fast enough. Not by a long shot. Fargo took two quick bounds and slammed the Henry's stock against the man's temple, felling Hardwick like a poled ox.

Zeke and the fourth owl hoot backed off, not wanting any part of him. But Grifter lunged, his brawny arms outstretched, sadistic glee curling his thin lips. He thought that he had Fargo dead to rights. He was wrong.

Shifting, the Trailsman rammed the barrel into Grifter's gut. Grifter doubled over, flushing scarlet, his lungs expelling a breath in a loud *whoosh*. Clutching his abdomen, he tottered, spittle flecking his chin.

"How about you two?" Fargo said to Zeke and the fourth man. Both vigorously shook their heads, Zeke's eyelids fluttering more madly than before.

Grifter did not know when he was well off. Jabbing a finger, he snarled, "No one does that to me and gets away with it! No one! By the time I'm through, you'll beg me to put you out of your misery, you rotten son of a—"

The cutthroat got no further. Fargo swung the Henry in a tight arc, the stock catching Grifter squarely on the cheek and splitting it like an overripe melon. Grifter staggered, blood spurting. A roar of white-hot rage spewed from his throat. Forgetting himself, the big ruffian lunged again. This time Fargo brought the stock up and around, smashing it against Grifter's jaw. Teeth crunched. Grifter's head was jolted backward and he rocked on his heels. Then, like melting wax, the hothead oozed to the earth, unconscious.

"Lordy!" Zeke said. "I ain't ever seen anybody get the better of Tom before."

"That makes two of us," said the fourth man, awed.

Fargo backed off, the Henry steady at his side. "When he comes around, tell him he's welcome to look me up any time he wants." Fargo nodded to the west, at a cluster of boulders. Four mounts waited there. "Tote your friends over and throw them on their horses."

Zeke meekly complied. "Whatever you say, friend. Just don't do to me what you did to Tom. I ain't got all that many teeth left as it is." To demonstrate, he opened his mouth wide, revealing a gap where several of his lower front ones had been. Those on the top were yellow or dark with rot. "It's gettin' so, I'll be gummin' my food before I'm fifty."

Zeke took hold of Grifter's wrists, the other man picked up the legs, and working together they shuffled toward their animals, going from boulder to boulder in order not to expose themselves to the woman up the canyon. After draping their burden over a dun, they returned for Hardwick.

"Damn," Zeke groused as he puffed along like a steam engine. "I wish to blazes this varmint would quit eatin' so much. Any heavier, I'd pull a groin muscle."

Hoisting Hardwick onto his sorrel proved to be a challenge. Zeke and the fourth gunman strained and heaved and sputtered, Zeke sagging against the horse in relief when they finally succeeded. "Jehoshaphat! It's a wonder he can find britches that fit. I'd be downright embarrassed to go through life lookin' like one of those big bluefish with holes in the tops of their heads."

"They're called whales," Fargo said.

"That's them," Zeke confirmed. "Saw a couple once, when I was in California. They were blowin' and rollin' and havin' a grand old time." The beanpole scratched himself. "Almost made me wish I was one. I'll bet they don't have a care in the world."

Fargo pegged Zeke as one of those who jabbered worse than chipmunks. "Climb on and head out," he directed.

"What about our shooting irons and our rifles?" asked the last member of the foursome.

Zeke nodded. "Surely you ain't fixin' to have us wander around unarmed? Hell, ain't you heard that Mescaleros have been seen hereabouts recently? We'll lose our hides."

"I'll leave your guns right where they are," Fargo proposed. "In about an hour, you can come back and claim them." It was the best he could do. Allowing them to take their hardware invited a shot in the back once Grifter and Hardwick revived. Wagging the Henry, he shooed them on their way. Zeke, leading Grifter's mount, grinned and waved as if they were the best of friends.

Fargo did not budge until they were well out of the canyon and bearing to the south. Then, pivoting, he jogged to the huge boulder. Leaning against it, he called out, "Lady! I'm a friend. Did you hear those horses leave? The men who were giving you a hard time are gone. It's safe to come out."

The woman did not reply. Fargo repeated himself, adding, "I'm not out to hurt you. I'm riding dispatch for the army and just happened by."

Silence reigned. Fargo wondered if maybe the woman had been hit and was lying out there somewhere, bleeding to death. Sidling to where he could see up the canyon, he spied a horse on its side forty yards away. A spreading crimson pool explained why. Grifter and his friends must have shot it out from under her.

"Ma'am? Can you hear me?" Fargo tried one more time.

"I hear you just fine," said a low, sultry voice to his rear. "Now be so kind as to put down that rifle and raise your arms."

"But I'm not out to—" Fargo began, turning, and was riveted to the spot by the sharp retort of a pistol and the *spang* of a slug off the boulder by his shoulder. He did as she had requested.

"You learn quick," the woman said. "Who are you?" she asked suspiciously. "How can you claim to be a soldier when you're not wearing a uniform?"

"I never claimed I was *in* the army," Fargo clarified. "I like my freedom too much. I could never stand still for always having someone tell me what to do." As he spoke, Fargo slowly faced her. He did not know what he expected, but certainly not to find a stunning blonde whose alluring eyes were a richer shade of blue than his own. She was dressed in scuffed boots, baggy pants, and a loose shirt that hid the contours of her body. A battered black hat crowned her golden mane. Around her slender waist was strapped a cartridge belt. In her right hand, fixed on her chest, was a cocked Smith & Wesson.

"What's your handle?" the beauty demanded.

The Trailsman told her. "I'm carrying a dispatch to Cantonment Burgwin." The post had been built eight years ago by the 1st U.S. Dragoons to protect the Taos Valley from Apaches and Utes. Never officially designated a fort, it was due to close in a few weeks. "Your name is Cambridge?" he prodded.

"Ivy Cambridge," the blonde confirmed. "I was on my way to Sumner's Trading Post when Grifter and his pack of polecats bushwhacked me. Damn them all to hell."

"What were they after?" Fargo asked.

Ivy shrugged. "What do you think?" she said. "I'm a female, aren't I?"

There was no denying that. Despite the bulky clothes, she had a sensual allure that turned Fargo's thoughts to wondering how she would look in clothes that fit. Put her in a tight dress and spruce up her hair and she would be a whole new woman. But Fargo doubted that her being female had anything to do with why she was waylaid. Still, if that was what she wanted him to believe, so be it.

"I'd be obliged if we could ride double as far as Cantonment Burgwin," Ivy said. "I can pick up a new horse there and ride on back to fetch my saddle and bedroll. What do you say?"

"I'll go you one better," Fargo said. "We'll rig up a travois to carry your gear."

"A what?"

"You'll see." Fargo pointed to the Smith & Wesson. "So can I move? Or do you intend to keep me covered all the way to the post?"

Cambridge twirled the revolver into her holster with a flourish that would have done any savvy gunhand proud. Patting the smooth butt, she said, "Just remember. I know how to use this. Any shenanigans and I'll give you some lead pills for what ails you."

Fargo laughed, sincerely liking her brash nature. Women on the frontier were generally a tougher lot than their city-bred sisters. They had to be, what with hostiles and wild beasts and white men who were little better than beasts themselves. Country gals did not tolerate nonsense. And any man who tried to take advantage was asking to eat his own teeth. "Don't fret," he assured her. "I know how to behave."

"Do you indeed?" Ivy said skeptically. "If so, you're one of a rare breed, Mr. Fargo. Most men can't keep their hands off a pretty woman if their lives depend on it." She paused, gazing in the direction the four hardcases had taken. "Tom Grifter is a prime example. The man thinks God gave him the right to ride roughshod over any female he wants."

"That sounds like experience talking," Fargo noted.

The blonde scowled and changed the subject. "So what in the world is a travois, anyhow? That's a new one on me."

Obviously, she had never lived among the Plains tribes, or among the Indians who called the northern Rockies their home. Travois were commonly used to transport lodges, parfleches, and other belongings.

Fargo related as much as he scoured their vicinity for two long limbs. Trees, though, were few and far between. He had to settle for four short branches chopped off a stunted pine. Rope sufficed to lash them into pairs long enough to serve as the frame for the platform. Trimming enough smaller limbs to fashion the platform at one end of the makeshift poles took about half an hour.

The sun was high in the sky when Fargo tied the opposite ends of the poles to the Ovaro's saddle. Ivy's saddle and bedroll were secured on the travois. Her saddlebags she insisted on slinging over a shoulder.

They were set to leave. Stepping to the dead mare, Ivy regarded the animal in quiet respect for a bit, then gave it the highest compliment any mount could receive. "She never gave me cause to complain. I feel wrong, leaving her for the scavengers like this."

Fargo tilted his head skyward. Already half a dozen buzzards were circling. Soon there would be three times as many. By nightfall coyotes would show up, or maybe a mountain lion would catch wind of the blood and investigate. In three days there would be little left of the mare except bones and a pool of dry blood. "Let's get going while we have some daylight left," he said.

Ivy had to climb on first, carefully sliding her legs over the poles and making herself as comfortable as she could. Fargo forked leather and clucked to the pinto. Neither of them had a word to say until they came to a steep gully Fargo could not go around. As they angled down the slope, the stallion gave a lurch. Ivy was thrown against Fargo's back, her bosom mashing against his shoulder blades.

"Sorry," she bleated.

"No need to be," Fargo said. "You'd better hold on. I want to put as many miles behind us as I can." He had planned on reaching the post by the middle of the next morning. Now it would be late in the afternoon, or early evening. Which meant the two of them had to spend the night together.

Not that Fargo indulged in any frisky notions. Ivy Cambridge kept one hand on her six-shooter at all times. She rode easily, relaxed, at home on horseback, indicating she had spent a lot of time in the saddle. A faint hint of perfume mingled with her natural earthy scent to tingle Fargo's nostrils. The warm feel of her body on his back and the caress of her breath on his neck was enough to prickle his skin from head to toe.

Over an hour went by without Ivy Cambridge saying a word. Fargo did not pester her with questions about where she was from or what she was doing in that neck of the woods. It was none of his business. Prying was a bad habit of those who were too full of themselves for their own good.

Besides, Fargo was accustomed to being quiet. Traveling alone for days or even weeks at a time, as he often did, gave a person a whole new appreciation for golden silence.

Ivy cleared her throat. "I never did thank you for coming to my rescue back yonder. If you hadn't shown up when you did, those boys might have made wolf meat of me."

"Maybe," Fargo said. "But I'd bet my poke that you would have taken a few of them with you."

Her laughter rippled like the bubbling of a frosty mountain stream. "You're a shrewd judge of character, Mr. Fargo. Yes, I would do my damnedest to make those bastards pay. I'd like to leave this old world the same way I came into it, kicking and screaming."

"You're shy of them now," Fargo reminded her. "If they have any brains at all, they won't badger you again."

"You wouldn't say that if you knew Grifter as well as I do."

Just then, almost as if on cue, the crack of a rifle shattered the stillness. Twisting, Fargo saw the four cutthroats bearing down at a gallop, rifles pressed to their shoulders. In the center was Tom Grifter, his battered and swollen face lit by hellish savagery.

"We've got them now, boys! Cut them down, horse and all!"

2

Skye Fargo's Henry leaped from its scabbard as he yanked
and twisted. He could not outrun the killers, not with the
stallion burdened by the travois. To try and reach cover
with the quartet bearing down would be a costly mistake.
He had to make a stand then and there.

Fixing a hasty bead on the foremost rider, who happened
to be the cutthroat whose name he had not learned, the
Trailsman held his breath a moment to steady his aim, then
fired. At the *blam* of the .44-caliber rifle, the hardcase catapulted backward as if smashed in the forehead by a sledge-
hammer.

Instantly, Grifter and the other two veered to either side.
Hardwick snapped off a shot that buzzed high, while Zeke
ducked low over his saddle and bolted toward some
mesquite. Grifter did what he usually did when he was
mad; he swore a blue streak.

Ivy Cambridge had a rifle, too, a fancy English model
complete with a sling. It had been pinned under her mare
back at the canyon. Now it was slung over her shoulder.
Unlimbering it, she swiveled to bring it to bear on Grifter.
Her shot provoked another outburst of cuss words. Before
she could fire again, Grifter was lost in dense brush. "We
can't stay in the open," she said.

Fargo goaded the Ovaro into a brisk walk. The travois
rattled and bounced, threatening to fall apart if they went

any faster. The bang of Ivy's rifle was reassuring. She was keeping the human wolves at bay. Only Hardwick was still in the open, and he was swiftly retreating out of range.

"They won't come at us like that again," Ivy gloated.

"No, now they'll try to backshoot us," Fargo said. They needed to find somewhere they could hold Grifter's men off. Occasional shots from the rear spurred him to a dry wash. An earthen ramp, formed when part of the wall had buckled, gave him the means of taking the pinto to the bottom.

Reining up, Fargo swung Ivy Cambridge to the ground. Her attention was behind them, and she gave a start when his arm looped around her slim waist. As he lowered her, they were chest to chest, almost chin to chin. No amount of baggy clothes could hide the fact that she was soft and warm and shapely in all the right places. As her feet touched the ground, a smile touched her full lips.

"Thanks."

Fargo slid down and scooted to the rim they had just vacated. None of the killers were visible. Zeke was to the southwest somewhere, Grifter to the northwest, Hardwick roughly in the middle.

"This is as good a spot as any," Ivy said, surveying the area. "They can't get at us without crossing thirty feet of open ground. We can pick them off like flies."

Fargo indicated a spindle of brush much closer than thirty feet. "What about there? If they reach it, we're in trouble." He pointed to the north, where boulders littered the rim above a sharp bend. "Or there?"

"At least we have some cover." Ivy persisted. "What else would you have us do? Untie the travois and leave my saddle and bedroll here for them to destroy? Because that's exactly what Grifter would relish. The man is so full of spite, it oozes out his ears."

"I have an idea," Fargo said. "Instead of lying here waiting to be picked off, we take the fight to them."

"How's that?"

"Stay put, and don't let anything happen to my horse."
Turning before she could object, Fargo sprinted northward
to the bend. Scrambling up the side of the boulders, he hid
and scanned the flatland for sign of the badmen. A hint of
movement rewarded his patience. Hardwick was seventy
yards out, on his hands and knees in some sage, creeping
along like an oversized gila monster.

Fargo sighted down the Henry. As his finger curled
around the trigger, Hardwick inexplicably flattened. Fargo
held his fire. He was not about to advertise where he was
unless he had a clear shot to make it worthwhile.

Suddenly several small birds, sparrows, fluttered from
stunted trees to the southwest. Zeke did not show himself,
but Fargo had his position marked.

Grifter was the only one unaccounted for, and Fargo did
not like that one bit. There was no predicting what the man
would do. Grifter was the most bloodthirsty of the bunch, a
lobo who slaughtered people and horses alike for the sheer
thrill of spilling blood. It made him the most dangerous.

Killing Grifter could well convince the others that they
should light a shuck for parts unknown. But try as Fargo
might, he failed to locate him. For all of Grifter's swagger
and bluster, he could move through undergrowth with the
skill of an Apache. Well, maybe a Pima.

For over a minute nothing happened. All was quiet. Then
Ivy's English rifle boomed. An answering squawk rose
from the brush concealing Zeke. An arm flopped into view
and disappeared again. Dry limbs crackled and snapped as
Zeke barreled to a new position.

Fargo shook his head. The man had no business riding
with the likes of Grifter and Hardwick. Zeke was nowhere
near as coldhearted as those two, as he had demonstrated

by wanting to put Ivy's mare out of its misery. To compound matters, Zeke was as stealthy as a bull buffalo and as clumsy as a two-year-old. It would be better for the scarecrow if he hung up his pistol and took up pushing pencils for a living, or strapped himself behind a plow. Zeke would live longer.

The slight shake of Fargo's head proved to be a mistake. He was searching for Hardwick when a rifle belched lead and smoke, to his right. The slug ricocheted off a boulder close to his left ear. Stinging shards drew blood. Fargo dropped, mentally chiding himself for being an idiot. Another inch or so, and Ivy Cambridge would be on her own.

At least Fargo now had a general idea of where Grifter was. Snaking forward, he came to a boulder as big around as a stagecoach wheel. Rising onto his knees, he removed his hat before bending an eye to the edge.

Not so much as a leaf stirred in the chaparral. The killers had learned from their mistakes. Even Zeke. Fargo saw Ivy's pretty face poke above the wash rim; she glanced both ways, and then dipped below it again. If she kept that up, she would have her head blown off.

One of the curly wolves shared his sentiments. Again Ivy rose to scour the brush. This time a rifle blasted. The bullet tore into the dirt in front of her, kicking some into her eyes, and she flung herself backward.

Puffs of gunsmoke pinpointed the shooter. It was Hardwick, now fifty yards out, sheltered by yucca. Or so he thought. Pumping the Henry's lever, Fargo sent five rapid shots into the vegetation. Whether he scored or not was impossible to say.

The next second both Grifter *and* Zeke joined the fray, firing at the smoke from Fargo's Henry. He hugged the dry soil, dust getting into his nose every time he inhaled, as lead screamed and whizzed. They fired ten times, all told, showing him that they had plenty of ammunition.

Ivy answered their shots, her English model roaring louder than the other. Grifter and his men responded in kind, and for five minutes the air rocked to the constant crash of rifles.

Fargo took advantage of the din. Backing up, he crawled to the other side of the boulder and on through a wide belt of weeds to heavier brush.

In a crouch, he slanted to the right in a wide loop that brought him up behind the three cutthroats. By then the firing had tapered off. Pausing, he listened for telltale evidence of where they were. But they were being canny now and did not give themselves away. Accordingly, he went on the prowl for Grifter, the leader.

Ten minutes of fruitless hunting left Fargo stumped. He'd had a general idea of where Grifter had gone to ground. Was he mistaken? Or had Grifter gone elsewhere while he was circling?

The muffled snap of a twig reminded Fargo of the other two. Blending into the chaparral, he crept toward the source. It had to be Hardwick. Or so he assumed until he spotted Zeke moving away from him. The three renegades were changing positions right and left.

Fargo was beginning to think they had no wilderness savvy whatsoever when a faint sound behind him caused him to turn just as a steel blade sheared at the small of his back. He dodged it, but barely.

Hardwick had reared up out of a patch of mesquite barely broad enough to hide a child. The man had more skill than Fargo gave him credit for. Batting the Henry aside with his free hand, Hardwick thrust the knife down low.

Fargo had to let go of the rifle to save himself. He grabbed Hardwick's wrist with both hands, stopping the keen tip a whisker's width from his groin. Pivoting, he wrenched on Hardwick's right arm and stuck his boot in front of Hardwick's legs. The result was predictable. Hardwick tumbled, but he was upright with amazing speed, a human cat, for all his bulk.

Fargo snatched at his Colt. The heavyset hardcase closed in, flicking at his hand. His skin pricked, and a trickle of blood appeared. Sidestepping, he evaded a swipe that would have cut him to the rib bones.

Hardwick pressed in closer to keep Fargo from resorting to the six-shooter. His knife weaved an intricate pattern of slashes, jabs, and sweeping blows intended to sever Fargo's jugular. It was all Fargo could do to avoid them, let alone pull his gun.

They danced through the growth, Fargo seeking to put bushes between them, Hardwick constantly pressing, pressing, pressing. A whang on Fargo's buckskin shirt was clipped. Another slicing shimmer nicked Fargo's shoulder.

Fargo had to do something, pronto. When Hardwick speared the steel at his chest, he feinted to the left. Immediately, Hardwick rotated on the balls of his feet and lanced the razor point at his heart. But Fargo was already reversing himself, throwing his body to the right so that he wound up at Hardwick's elbow, and slightly behind him.

Throwing out his arms, Fargo clamped them around the killer's own, pinning them so Hardwick could not wield the blade. Hardwick threw himself every which way in a violent attempt to toss Fargo off, but Fargo clung to him like glue.

It was a temporary stalemate, at best.

The padding around Hardwick's thick waist was no true measure of his immense strength. He was like an incensed mule, bucking and kicking and trying to gouge Fargo with his elbows and butt Fargo with the back of his head. It was akin to trying to hold a whirlwind. A whirlwind that weighed upward of three hundred pounds.

Fargo heaved backward, seeking to tug Hardwick off his

feet and throw the man to the ground. But Hardwick would not budge; he was an oak when he rooted himself. Stymied, Fargo hooked a leg around Hardwick's left ankle and flung them both forward. He wanted to trip the cutthroat. Somehow, though, Hardwick twisted sharply while kicking outward with his imprisoned ankle.

The result was that Fargo found himself on his back, with a living mountain blotting out a sizeable portion of the sky above him. Polished steel gleamed in a stray shaft of sunlight. He rolled to the left as the knife arced in a glittering stab meant to impale him.

Fargo felt a stinging sensation along his back. He heard Hardwick grunt. Pushing to his knees, he brought up both hands in time to ward off a kick. As he shot erect, Hardwick's left hand flashed toward his face. Dirt caught him in the mouth, in the nose, in the eyes.

Tears blurred Fargo's vision. Frantically, he backpedaled, unable to see a blessed thing. Vegetation clawed at his legs, nearly tripping him. He had no idea where Hardwick was until the killer indulged in a gruff chortle.

"I've got you now, you slippery bastard."

Dabbing at his eyes, Fargo blinked again and again and again in a vain bid to clear them. The world was an awful blur. He heard a shuffling step and focused his other senses. His ears registered Hardwick's heavy breathing. Whirling toward the sound, he retreated, throwing one leg out behind him after the other, fearful of tripping and giving Hardwick an easy victory.

"Scared yet, mister?" the killer taunted. "You should be. I'm going to gut you and string your innards all over creation to draw the buzzards. You'll die slow and painful for bucking us."

Vague shapes materialized. Dimly, Fargo could distinguish Hardwick's silhouette, but not much else. His hearing

27

had to compensate for his eyes awhile longer yet. The crunch of a twig alerted him to a sudden thrust. He skipped to one side, his hands close to his waist to keep from having his fingers hacked off.

"Damn, you're worse than a gopher snake," Hardwick grumbled. His bulky form spurted forward.

Fargo retreated once again. Only this time he backed into a tall bush that would not yield. Its branches clung to him like scores of tiny claws. He tried to shift to the left and could not. Tears streamed over his cheeks and down his chin, but still his vision would not clear.

"I have you!" Hardwick boasted.

Shadows separated, swirled. Abruptly, Fargo could see the gunman and the blade streaking at his throat. He jerked his neck to the right. The knife missed, but so close did it come that the blade brushed the surface of his skin and left a thin red smear in its wake.

Hardwick was beside himself. "Hold still, damn you!" he roared.

Did the man really expect Fargo to stand there as meekly as a little lamb and be cut to ribbons? Whipping a fist up and in, Fargo connected. His knuckles pulped Hardwick's nose. The cutthroat bellowed like a bull in torment and backed off, covering his nostrils with his left hand.

"You broke it! I'll cut yours off for this! See if I don't!"

Hardwick talked too much. He gloated when he should slash, taunted when he should thrust. Many bullies and roughnecks had the same fault. They let their mouths do their fighting.

Fargo never did. If there was one lesson he had learned during his days with the Sioux and in countless clashes since, it had to be that there was a proper time and place for everything. Just as a Bible puncher had once told him, there was a time to love and a time to hate, a time to laugh and a time to mourn, a time to talk and a time to shut up and fight like hell.

The killer hiked his knife in both hands. His beady eyes shone with raw malice.

Uncoiling like a panther, Fargo punched him. Not on the jaw or in the face. Not in the gut or the ribs. No, Fargo punched Hardwick in the *throat* with all his might.

Gasping, Hardwick recoiled. Blinking as Fargo had done moments earlier, he sucked in a ragged breath. Gagging, he staggered backward. His features were a mask of disbelief. The knife was forgotten as he clasped a hand to his crushed larynx.

Unnoticed, Fargo palmed the Colt. His thumb curled back the hammer as he drew. Hardwick saw, and sputtered, and blanched. At a range of no more than six inches, Fargo fired.

For long seconds the killer's head was wreathed in swirling gunsmoke. When the breeze blew the smoke away, Hardwick was prone, blank eyes fixed on uncaring clouds.

Fargo crouched. The shot was bound to lure Grifter and Zeke. Spying the Henry, he hastened toward it. Here in the brush he would rather rely on the long gun than the revolver. The reason was not hard to fathom. The Henry Lever-Action Cartridge Magazine Rifle, as it was officially called, could shoot farther with greater penetration and more pure knockdown force.

Another plus was the number of rounds the Henry held. No gun ever made, no other rifle or carbine or musket or flintlock or pistol, ever held fifteen bullets at once. An experienced shootist could squeeze off thirty rounds in a minute. Small wonder that some folks had taken to calling the Henry the gun a person "could load on Sunday and shoot all blamed week."

Concealed in mesquite, Fargo waited for the other two. He could not understand why they did not show. Grifter he might not hear, but Zeke was bound to make enough racket to raise the dead.

"Hardwick, did you take care of him?"

Grifter's shout came from the east. Fargo whirled, his cheek tucked to the Henry. It surprised him that Grifter would be so careless. Sliding to the left, he hunted a target. Unless his ears deceived him, Grifter was near the dry wash. He was tempted to call out to Ivy Cambridge to verify she was all right, but common sense persuaded him not to.

Muted voices rose in anger. Fargo thought he recognized Grifter's. There was a faint noise, as of a hand slapping a cheek.

"Fargo? Skye Fargo? Can you hear me?"

The Trailsman was jarred. How had Grifter learned who he was?

"Sweet little Ivy here tells me that's your handle," Grifter bellowed. "You'd best answer me, mister, before I do something you're likely to regret."

Was it a trick? Fargo mused. He was gazing toward the wash and saw Ivy's head pop up. She appeared to be fine. Then she rose higher, exposing herself from the waist up. He was about to straighten and motion for her to get out of sight when another figure reared directly behind her.

Tom Grifter had a pistol jammed against her temple. From the way her shoulder was hunched and the discomfort on her face, he had hold of her by the right wrist, which he had twisted up behind her back. "Did you think I was bluffin', friend?" he hollered. "Show yourself or I'll give her a new ear hole."

Ever so slowly, Fargo unfurled. Without being bidden, he advanced, settling a bead on Grifter's shoulder. It was not much of a shot but it was the best he could do with Grifter using Ivy as a human shield. "Let the woman go! This is between the two of us."

"Shows how much you know!" Grifter responded. "Ivy and me go back a long way." Leering, he roughly shook her. "Ain't that right, honey? Tell the man how much I mean to you."

Judging by the blonde's expression, she would like nothing better than to pump five or six slugs into him.

"Come closer, big man," Grifter directed, "so I don't need to shout."

Fargo did so, hoping all the while that the killer would show more of himself. But Grifter was too smart. As Fargo strode into the open, the hardcase ducked down. The only part of him that Fargo could see was his forearm.

"That's far enough! Now drop that shiny Henry of yours. And the Colt, too, while you're at it."

Fargo was not about to do either. Grifter would shoot him, then slay Ivy and take whatever he wanted. Keeping his sights centered on the outlaw's arm, he took a few more steps.

"Didn't you hear me?" Grifter railed. "Lower the damn gun this second or I'll splatter her brains all over this wash! I'm not bluffin'!"

Fargo halted, but he did not let the barrel drop. Ivy Cambridge gave him a probing look, as if she were trying to let him know that it was all right for him to go ahead and shoot, that it was fine by her. But it was not fine by him.

"I don't believe you!" Grifter huffed, peering past Ivy's right ear. "Don't you care what happens to her? Don't you give a damn whether she lives or dies?"

Fargo did, but he would never admit as much. So long as Grifter was unsure, Ivy stood a chance. "Your best bet is to take what you want and clear out."

Grifter's eyes widened. "Did you hear that?" he addressed Ivy. "I'm holdin' a gun to *your* head, and he's tellin' *me* what I should do! Where do you find these lunatics, anyhow? Do you put a notice in the newspaper?"

"Go to hell," Ivy said.

Fargo started to slide to the right. A couple of feet, and he would have a clear shot. He stopped cold, however, when Zeke rose from the wash a few yards from the blonde and her tormentor. Zeke's rifle was trained on his abdomen.

"Shoot him, Zeke," Grifter commanded.

"Can't, cousin," the beanpole said, his eyelids doing their butterfly imitation.

"Why not, you half-wit? Do I need to paint a bull's-eye on his chest?"

"His rifle might go off and hit Missy Cambridge."

Grifter was so upset, his gun hand shook with fury. "If you weren't kin, I'd plug you my own self." Glaring wildly, he backed into the wash, hauling Ivy after him. "Now I got no choice. Cover me while I fetch the saddlebags. Then we're gettin' out of here."

Zeke timidly smiled at Fargo. "Sorry about all this bother, mister. But when Tom gets his dander up, he's a ring-tailed snorter. Don't fret, though. He's not about to hurt Missy."

There was a commotion below. "Come on! I have it!" Grifter bawled.

Nodding farewell, Zeke whisked into the wash as if his hind end were ablaze. Pounding footsteps dwindled, and Fargo rushed to the rim. Below stood Ivy Cambridge, strangely grinning. To the south, just vanishing around a turn, were Zeke and Tom Grifter, the latter clutching saddlebags.

"So they got what they wanted, after all," Fargo said.

"They think they did," Ivy responded. Stepping to a cleft, she reached in and pulled out a pair of saddlebags. "These are mine. I hid them right after you snuck off."

Fargo glanced down the wash. "Then whose—?"

"They took yours."

3

Two hours later Fargo was still annoyed.

They had covered more territory before dark set in and made camp in an oval basin. A tiny spring slaked their thirst. Ivy Cambridge gathered wood for the fire while Fargo untied the travois and stripped the Ovaro.

Since Fargo's few personal effects had all been in his saddlebags, including his small coffeepot and supply of coffee, they had to go without. The same with the pemmican and jerky he ordinarily carried.

"What about you?" Fargo asked the blonde, pointing at her saddlebags. "Anything in there we can eat?"

"Nothing," Ivy said curtly, clasping them close as if afraid he would try to take them from her.

It was peculiar. Just as peculiar as her habit of never letting her saddlebags out of her sight. Where she went, they went, even when she gathered firewood.

Fargo had to admit that he was curious to learn what Grifter had been after, but he did not demand to see inside. While he kindled the fire, she spread out their blankets. His went on one side, hers on the other. So much for the notion he was harboring of maybe getting to see exactly what those bulky clothes hid.

They had to do without supper. For all Fargo knew, Grifter and Zeke were in the area and would hear any shots that brought down game. The pair were bound to come after them once Grifter discovered he had swiped the wrong saddlebags.

Ivy Cambridge hardly said four words all evening. After a while she took a small leather-bound notebook from a shirt pocket, and a short pencil. Licking the latter, she flipped pages until she came to the one she wanted and began to write.

Just to have something to talk about, Fargo asked, "What's that?"

"My diary."

Fargo's brow puckered. He had heard tell of young girls keeping diaries, but never grown women. "Must help you pass time on the trail," he observed.

Writing slowly, the pink tip of her tongue poking from the corner of her mouth, Ivy did not respond right away. "It's more than that. Writing everything down helps me sort out my thoughts, my feelings. I can look back and see I'm not quite as bad off as I was when I started it."

What did that mean? Fargo wondered. Now that she had opened up to him a little, he tried to keep the conversation going. "Have any family in New Mexico?"

"My ma and pa are long dead. My sister died of smallpox when I was eight. My brother drowned when I was twelve. The only other relative I have, an aunt, lives in New York City. She wants nothing to do with me. Says I'm tainted. That my ma should never have married my no-account pa."

"Sounds like you're better off without her," Fargo said.

Ivy looked away, into the distance. A sorrowful expression came over her, so profoundly sad that for a moment Fargo expected her to burst into tears. But her jaw firmed, her lips thinned, and she resumed writing.

The mystery deepened. Here was a woman with a fancy eastern name, but one who acted and talked more like a country gal than a city vixen. And her clothes! The only

other woman Fargo had ever met who wore such baggy attire was a hellcat with the unlikely name of Maple Juniper
Rose, and the only reason Maple did it was to disguise her
gender so she could mingle with the troops at various forts.
She had a fondness for men that rivaled her fondness for
hard liquor.

Maple Rose liked to brag that she could "outride, out-
shoot, and outscrew any man alive." And from what Fargo
had been told, it was no idle boast. He'd never been
tempted by her charms himself, but he knew others who
had. One young recruit had taken four days to recover.

Fargo took a branch, broke it in two, and added both
pieces to the flames. To take Ivy's mind off whatever had
upset her, he remarked, "You must have a lucky man somewhere."

"I hate men."

The venom in her tone startled Fargo. "We're not all that
bad," he tried to joke.

"That's a matter of opinion," Ivy said while scrawling.

"Sooner or later the right one will come along and
change your outlook," Fargo ventured. He was only trying
to be friendly, but she snapped the diary shut and jabbed
the pencil at him as if she hankered to bury it in his eye.

"Listen closely. I want nothing to do with men. Ever. If
any man ever lays a hand on me in the wrong way, I'll chop
off his oysters and shove them down his throat." Ivy
paused. "Have I made myself clear?"

"Yes, ma'am."

"Good. Now quit bothering me. When I have an urge to
chat, you'll be the second one to know." Replacing the
small notebook, she crawled under her blankets and curled
up on her side with her back to him.

Fargo could take a hint. If that was how she wanted to
be, fine. He would not waste his breath arguing differently.
There were plenty of females around who were fond of the

male species, and as soon as he reached a town, he was going to rustle one up and remind himself of exactly why he liked women so much.

He stayed awake until almost midnight, partly to insure that Grifter and Zeke did not pay them a visit, partly to relish the night sounds of the desert. Coyotes yipped long and loud. Birds screeched. Twice cougars screamed like women in labor.

Once, early on, a throaty rumbling growl issued from the darkness, a growl such as a grizzly would make. Only there were no grizzlies that far south, leading him to suspect it was a jaguar. The big cats sometimes prowled well north of the Mexican border, slaughtering sheep and cattle. He built the fire up but did not spot it. Later he heard another growl, much farther away.

After turning in, he tossed and turned, unable to get to sleep. Why, he could not say. Sometimes coffee would keep him awake, but he had not had any. It couldn't be the loss of the saddlebags, he told himself. Every item in them could be replaced at the first general store he came to.

He wound up facing the fire, and Ivy Cambridge. She had not stirred all night. Either she was the soundest sleeper he had ever encountered, or she was shamming, not willing to go to sleep until he did. Several times he had felt as if he were being watched, but when he looked up she was always in the same position.

Long about three in the morning, Fargo gratefully dozed. He meant to be up at first light, but it was warm sunshine on his face that awakened him. The sun had risen half an hour ago. Sitting up, he went to stretch and saw Ivy already awake, her knees tucked to her chest, staring at him. "Why didn't you get me up? We could have covered four or five miles by now."

"You needed your sleep."

Fargo shoved off his blanket and stood. How did she

know that, unless she had been awake the whole time? The new day was beginning exactly as the old one had ended. "I'll saddle up and rig the travois."

Presently, they were under way. As the sun climbed and the temperature rose, Fargo loosened his bandanna and pulled his hat low. He took it for granted that Ivy would be as talkative as she had been the day before, so he was mildly surprised when she asked a question out of the blue.

"How about you? Is there a lucky woman somewhere?"

"No," Fargo admitted. "It will be years before I'm ready to settle down, if ever."

"Oh. You're one of those who likes to kiss and run, who treats women as if they are playthings to dally with as you please."

Fargo glanced at her over his shoulder. "I won't deny that I'm fond of women, yes. I like the way they move, the way they smell, the way they feel." He could not help but grin when she sniffed in disdain. "And it might shock you to learn, lady, that there are women who are just as fond of men."

"Saloon girls, you mean," Ivy said, much as someone might say "bubonic plague." "Soiled doves down on their luck. Victims for men to prey on."

"A lot of those doves like doing what they do. Dancing and drinking and having fun is all they're interested in."

"Fun? Is that what you call it when a woman parades around in a skimpy dress for men to paw her?"

"Some women like to parade, as you put it. Just as some men like to strut. If everyone was as prudish as you, there wouldn't be any human race." Fargo felt her stiffen, but he did not ease up. "Believe it or not, there are men *and* women who are happiest when they mingle. There are men and women who are as fond of making love as you are of that diary of yours."

"Such talk!" Ivy huffed. "You're certainly no gentleman."

"I never claimed to be." Fargo set her straight. "But I don't see where you have room to talk. It's not exactly ladylike to go around threatening to hack the privates off of any male who so much as looks at you crosswise."

Ivy shifted as if she were about to jump off. "You're crude, as well as no gentleman. Typical. I don't know why I thought you might be a little different than the rest. A little better, maybe."

"I'm who I am and I don't make any bones about it," Fargo declared. "If I were as bad as you make me out to be, I would have tried to get in your pants last night. But I didn't, did I? No real man would."

"Is there some other kind?"

Fargo nodded. "There are men who act like boys, men who never quite grew up, men who treat women just the way you hate. A real man doesn't paw women. A real man doesn't force women against their will. A real man has the same respect for a lady that a lady has for him."

Ivy was silent for quite a spell. "I suppose you have a point," she conceded, "but if you ask me, there are more boys running around disguised as men than there are real men to be found."

"Keep looking. One day you'll find a real man of your own."

That shut her up for another hour. Fargo bore generally southward, the travois creaking louder than his saddle. A hot wind stirred dust devils but did little to cool him down. Whenever they came to a rise, he reined up and checked their back trail. As near as he could tell, they were not being followed.

Ivy's next question was as unexpected as her earlier one. "Why do you reckon God made men and women so different?"

Fargo laughed lightly. "Lady, you're asking the wrong person. Find a parson. He might know. Me, I'm just glad things are the way they are. Think of how boring it would be if everyone was the same."

For the first time since they met, Ivy Cambridge laughed. "I never thought of it quite like that. And I guess I shouldn't hold all men to blame for a few rotten apples. It's just that I've never met a truly good man before."

"Either you've set your sights too high, or you're looking in the wrong places. If Tom Grifter is an example of the company you keep, I'd say you need to expand your horizons."

"What about him?" Ivy said defensively.

"From the way he talked and acted, I got the impression that the two of you know one another fairly well. Am I right?"

Ivy answered in a tiny voice, barely audible. "Yes. We've met before. And I'll probably run into him again."

"Why? What is he after?"

It had been the natural thing to ask, but as soon as Fargo did, he realized he had made a mistake. The subject was taboo. Ivy clammed up and did not speak again the rest of the morning.

By noon they had reached the Rio Grande del Rancho, a confluent of the Rio Grande. Fargo rode on, briskly, eager to arrive at the post. Absently, he patted his buckskin shirt. Under it, strapped to his side, was the narrow pouch he was to deliver.

Fargo had taken to carrying dispatches on his person ever since the time he had been on dispatch duty in Montana and a flash flood had caught him flat-footed in a gully. The raging current had bowled the Ovaro over. He had clung to the saddle as the stallion righted itself and struggled to solid ground. Somehow, a saddlebag had come undone, and the dispatch had been swept away by the rushing waters. Ever since, Fargo kept them on him.

Insects droned noisily as the stallion paralleled the gurgling Rio Grande del Rancho. Fargo saw a yellow butterfly flit from flower to flower. Later three sandhill cranes flew by, headed southwest.

Just when Fargo least anticipated it, Ivy asked another question. And this one beat the others all hollow.

"Do you really like kissing and touching women?"

Fargo twisted, half convinced she was spoofing him. But no, she was in earnest. He had met some strange females in his wideflung travels, but it was safe to say that Ivy Cambridge ranked as one of the strangest. "That's like asking a bear if he's partial to honey. Or a bee if he's fond of nectar."

Ivy's face scrunched up as though she had bitten into a bitter root. "But all that pawing and squeezing and clawing. Doesn't it hurt them?"

"It's not like I rip their breasts off," Fargo said, making light of her worry. Then he glimpsed something in the depths of her eyes, something that hinted the topic was of supreme importance to her. Poker-faced, he added, "When a man and woman make love, it's not supposed to hurt. The idea is for you to enjoy it. Maybe some men get carried away and leave a bruise or two. But just as many women rip a man's back to shreds with their fingernails."

"I'd never do that."

"Not if you keep your nails clipped short, you won't," Fargo quipped. "You'll be doing the men in your life a favor."

"I told you before," Ivy said sternly, "I hate men. I'll never let a man touch me or kiss me ever again." She patted her revolver. "I've practiced with this hog leg until I can shoot off a man's dingus at fifty feet."

"That should come in real handy if you're attacked by a rabid pack of dinguses."

Ivy did not think much of his sense of humor. She clammed up again, averted her gaze, and pretended to be interested in the countryside.

Fargo let her be. The woman was severely troubled. By what, he could not guess, beyond the fact that it had something to do with men. Her claim to hate all males did not wash with him. She protested too much, as it were.

The afternoon waxed, the blazing orb above baking every living creature. Some adapted better than most. Birds roosted in what scant shade they could find. Bigger animals lay in their cool dens or burrows. Only lizards reveled in the heat, scampering here, there, and everywhere, zipping across the ground like scaly four-legged lightning bolts.

The *clang* of a blacksmith's hammer on an anvil let Fargo know that he was near his goal. Climbing to a low spine, he surveyed Cantonment Burgwin. Situated at the month of the Rito de la Olla, the post bustled with activity. It was hard to believe that in another two weeks not a living soul would be there.

Ivy was running a hand through her luxurious but tangled hair. "I wish I had a mirror. Mine broke when my mare took her spill." She bit her lower lip and said nervously, "All those soldiers."

Fargo bit his own lip to keep from laughing. This from the woman who claimed she hated men? Cambridge was a walking contradiction, in more ways than one. Clucking to the pinto, he meandered along the rutted truck that led to the post. No one challenged him. The sentries gave him the same bored look honed by sentries everywhere. Until the flowing golden hair of Ivy Cambridge caught their attention, that is.

Fargo reined up at a hitching post in front of the headquarters building. His travois had sparked almost as much interest as Ivy, who slid off without an assist from him and marched inside without so much as a word of thanks.

Dismounting, Fargo doffed his hat and slapped some of the dust from his buckskins. Reaching up under his shirt, he untied the cord that held the pouch in place. He went to put the cord in his saddlebags, forgetting they were gone. The door opened as he mounted the steps, and out walked a ramrod-stiff officer.

"Skye Fargo, as I live and breathe."

"Major Dexter, isn't it?" Fargo said. They had been acquainted briefly over a year ago on a campaign up north, where the major had come across as a no-nonsense career man with an abiding sense of fairness and duty. He shook Dexter's calloused hand. "No one told me you were in charge here."

"For another two weeks or so," the officer said rather regretfully. "Then it's off to Fort Riley and a damn desk job." Dexter ran a finger over his short waxed mustache. "It's a pity, really. Burgwin is ideally located and has proven invaluable in stemming the depredations of the Apaches. So naturally the army has decided that it should be closed down."

"I brought this," Fargo said, offering the dispatch. The major opened the pouch, extracted a single folded sheet of paper, and read the message.

"When it rains, it pours," Dexter said. "I've just been informed that the inspector general will be here the day before we're slated to close. He's to review the troops one final time, it says." Dexter snorted. "Who are they trying to fool? They don't trust me to oversee the closure, so he's been sent to guarantee I've done everything by the book."

Behind the major someone cleared a throat. "What about my request, Major?"

"Eh?" Dexter said, turning. "Oh. Miss Cambridge. Sorry. When I saw the Trailsman outside, I had to greet him." The officer folded the sheet. "I would prefer that you let me assign an escort. Please reconsider."

Ivy was studying Fargo as if they were complete strangers meeting for the very first time. "The Trailsman? You're the one folks talk about?"

"Only when they have nothing better to do," Fargo said. "It's all those tall tales made up by writers back East. If I ever catch one, I'll string him up by his thumbs and make him eat a few pages of his own words."

"Pshaw," Major Dexter said. "You're too modest, my friend." Clapping Fargo on the shoulder, he told Ivy, "You're looking at one of the finest scouts west of the Mississippi. There isn't an officer in the entire army who wouldn't give his eyeteeth to work with this man."

"And here I thought he was a worthless womanizer," Ivy said. Facing the officer, she said bluntly, "No escort. But what about my request? Can I have a horse or not?"

"Certainly, however—"

Ivy brushed by without another word and hurried toward the stable.

"Odd creature," Major Dexter said so only Fargo could hear.

"You know her?"

"Only by reputation. She shot a man in Santa Fe about eight months ago for taking undue liberties. Almost made a eunuch of him, as I understand." Dexter frowned. "Tough as she is, she has no business working for Frank Stockwell, and even less traveling alone with seven thousand dollars."

A feather could have floored Fargo. "Seven thousand?" So that was what she had in the saddlebags! A small fortune. A magnet for vermin like Tom Grifter and Hardwick. "Is she *loco*?"

"No. She's to deliver the money to Sumner's Trading Post by the end of the week, in time for the Great Footrace, as it's being billed."

"You've lost me."

Major Dexter leaned on the rail. "Don't tell me you've never heard of the annual Summer Footrace? It's held on May tenth, rain or shine, hot or cold. And this year promises to be a scorcher. The hot weather is here early, I'm afraid."

Fargo had not taken his eyes off Ivy Cambridge. "What is the seven thousand for?"

"What else? Prize money. Frank Stockwell works for one of the big newspapers. I can't recall which. Somehow or other he heard about the annual race. In the past the prize has always been a hundred dollars worth of credit at the trading post. But Stockwell had this brainstorm. Offer a lot of money, lure big crowds, make a major event out of it. Covered exclusively by his paper, of course."

"Of course," Fargo said. Ivy was talking to a sergeant. The noncom glanced toward the HQ and Major Dexter nodded. Ivy then led the sergeant into the stable.

The officer went on. "As a publicity gimmick, Stockwell hired Miss Cambridge to deliver the seven thousand overland. I imagine he'll write glowing accounts about her ordeals with hostiles and wild beasts and outlaws and the like."

"Does everyone in the territory know she's carrying the prize money?"

"Just about. Stockwell has been making the rounds of all the cities and towns, crowing about his illustrious enterprise, as he calls it. I'm surprised she made it this far."

"Doesn't Stockwell realize the danger he's put her in?"

"Whatever else Frank Stockwell might be, he's no fool. Yes, he realizes what he's done. And he doesn't care, so long as it supplies him with copy his readers will crave. I heard the man speak. He's a born opportunist if ever there was one."

Major Dexter elaborated, but Fargo barely heard. He was

thinking of the one hundred and sixty miles Ivy must cover to reach Sumner's Trading Post.

The sergeant stepped from the stable, swinging the left-hand door wide. Out rode Ivy on a fine dun. A flick of the reins, and she was off, trotting from the post and bearing southward.

Fargo was down the steps and untying the travois before the dun's dust settled. There was no rhyme or reason to what he was doing. He was acting on impulse.

"You're leaving so soon?" Major Dexter said. "I was ready to break out my private stock and swap war stories."

"Another time."

"You aren't by any chance heading south, are you?"

Skye Fargo did not reply. There was no need.

4

The woman could ride.

Fargo pushed hard, yet he had still not overtaken Ivy Cambridge when the sun dipped below the western horizon, painting brilliant dashes of red, yellow, and orange in the sky. He was beginning to understand why Stockwell had hired her. She truly could outride most any man alive.

Nightfall claimed New Mexico but Fargo rode on. Ivy was bound to make camp and he would soon spot her fire. Another half an hour passed with no sign of it. Then a full hour. He speculated that maybe she planned to ride the whole night through to make up for the time she had lost because of Grifter's ambush.

A minute later a pinpoint of light appeared, growing in size until Fargo could see individual flames licking the air and Ivy's bedroll spread out nearby. Her saddle was positioned to be her pillow. But Ivy herself was nowhere to be seen.

Reining up, Fargo waited for her to show herself. To ride right on in without hailing her might earn him a bullet in the skull. Or probably a lot lower down, considering what she had done to that frisky gent in Santa Fe.

When over five minutes elapsed, Fargo grew worried. Had Grifter got hold of her? Was she lying in the brush somewhere, dead or dying? Quietly sliding off the stallion, he snatched his Colt and stalked silently forward. Movement showed him where the dun was picketed.

Fargo circled the camp to stay out of the firelight. He was on the far side when faint noises wafted from the south. Splashing, it sounded like. Pines and heavy brush hid him as he crept to a point where he could see who or what was responsible.

They were in the foothills to the Sangre de Christo Range. A bubbling stream was ahead. Not far from the water's edge lay Ivy's clothes, boots, and hat. Closer still was her rifle, her gunbelt, and the saddlebags. In the center of a pool stood Ivy herself, as naked as the day she was born.

The sight took Fargo's breath away. Her skin glistened with vitality, a wet sheen accenting her shapely contours. For a moment she stood still, and it seemed to Fargo that he was gazing at a magnificent statue carved from solid marble, so exquisite was her body. Her shoulders were slender, her bosom ample. The tips of her breasts curled upward, enticing, the nipples hardened by the cold water. A flat stomach framed a pale triangle at the junction of alabaster thighs. She was a beauty from head to toe.

Her movements when she cupped water and splashed it on her chest were graceful and fluid. She was living poetry, the sort of woman who brought men on a street to a standstill, as lovely as any female ever born.

Fargo watched her wash her shoulders. The water trickled down over her breasts, around her glorious mounds and across her belly. Her hand followed it in lazy curves. When she arched her back in sensuous delight, her nipples thrust toward him and he felt a stirring in his loins.

Ivy tucked at the knees and sank under the surface. She was under only a few seconds. She emerged a goddess, sparkling and vibrant, the starlight casting her features in sharp relief. Running both hands over her wet hair, she hummed to herself.

This was the real Ivy Cambridge. An innocent in the wilderness. A woman who refused to admit her own beauty. A child afraid to grow up.

Or so Fargo assumed. She turned, and he tensed. High on her back were numerous small scars. He could not make out exactly how many, but there were a lot. She shifted again, denying him a good look.

Suddenly Ivy straightened and scrutinized the trees. Fargo held himself still, afraid she would spot him. She was bound to resent it and would want nothing more to do with him.

Ivy moved toward the bank, toward her weapons. She stopped with a hand stretched toward her rifle. Cocking her head, she listened, and when she did not hear anything out of the ordinary, she shrugged and waded into the pool again to resume her bath.

Fargo did not press his luck. Backing away, he skirted the camp. Just as he did, the wind shifted. The dun caught his scent and nickered loudly. He hurried on, knowing it would bring Ivy. Nor was he wrong. Within a minute of climbing back onto the Ovaro, she materialized across the clearing in her pants and partially buttoned shirt. Her boots were under her left arm, the gunbelt slung over a shoulder, the saddlebags over another. She scanned the area, the business end of her rifle ready to dispense death.

Fargo called out. "Don't shoot! I'm friendly." He walked the stallion close enough for Ivy to recognize him.

"Skye Fargo?" The barrel of her rifle did not lower. "What in tarnation are you doing here?" She paused. "You're shadowing me, you son of a bitch. You know about the prize money and you're waiting for a chance to get your hands on it."

"Trust me," Fargo said, boldly riding into the clearing.

"Your saddlebags are the last thing I want to have in my hands." Halting, he started to slip a boot from a stirrup.

"Hold on," Ivy said. "I haven't invited you into my camp. I've made it as plain as I know how that I want nothing to do with men. Can't you take a hint?"

Fargo folded his arms and grinned. "Why is it that whenever a man is the least bit friendly to a woman, she jumps to the conclusion that he wants to bed her? Not all men are lechers at heart." Which, on second thought, was a whopper of a lie if ever there was one. "Can I help it if we happen to be going in the same direction? I saw your fire and figured you wouldn't mind some company."

The decision was hers to make. Fargo would go if she insisted. Ivy shifted her weight from one foot to the other, gnawing on her lower lip as was her habit in times of stress. "Well, what will it be?" he prompted. "I spent most of the day hauling you and your saddle across half the territory, and I'm tired. I've earned some hot coffee and a good night's sleep."

The reminder did the trick. Ivy rested the stock of her rifle on the ground and said, "That's right. You did do me a big favor. I reckon I owe you." She gestured. "Climb down. I'll have coffee ready in two shakes of a lamb's tail."

"I'm obliged," Fargo said, feeling as if he had just won the grand prize at a carnival. Before leaving Cantonment Burgwin, he had bought new saddlebags and a few personal effects. Among them was a spanking new coffeepot and a new tin cup to replace the battered one he had packed along for a coon's age. He also purchased a new picket pin, which he now pounded into the ground using a rock. Patting the pinto, he joined Cambridge, his saddle and bedroll in hand.

Ivy pointed at a spot across the fire from her bedding, but Fargo dropped his gear near her blanket and proceeded to spread out his, heedless of the barbs her eyes shot at him.

"You do know about the prize money, don't you?" she would not let it rest.

"Major Dexter told me. If you ask my opinion—and you haven't—you're crazy to take the risk. Tom Grifter won't be the only hardcase after the seven thousand. It will be a miracle if you reach Sumner's Trading Post in one piece."

"I can take care of myself, thank you."

"Like you did against Grifter? If I hadn't come along when I did, your bones would be picked white by the buzzards by now." Placing his saddle on the edge of the blanket, Fargo sat and deposited the Henry and his new saddlebags.

"Tom wouldn't kill me. All he's interested in is the money."

"You're sure of that, are you?"

"I know him—" Ivy began, and did her clam imitation.

Not this time, Fargo thought. "How well? Well enough to sit there and look me in the eye and say that you would stake your life on it?" For a heartbeat she met his gaze, then she looked away. "I figured as much."

"You're just trying to scare me."

Fargo propped himself against his saddle. "You *should* be scared. Maybe you're right about Grifter. Maybe he wouldn't personally pull the trigger. But what about the others he brought along?"

"Zeke? He's as harmless as a little puppy. You saw. He'd never hurt me."

"I was thinking of Hardwick," Fargo said. "That sidewinder would have snuffed out your life as easily as he would a candle. Who's to say that Grifter didn't bring Hardwick along to do his dirty work for him?"

Ivy was severely troubled. "I never considered that," she confessed. "But why else would Tom partner up with a killer like him?"

Fargo stared intently at her face, studying the delicate

sweep of her arched brows, her fine aquiline nose and ruby lips. He stared for so long that she fidgeted.

"What the devil are you doing that for?"

"Strange. You don't *look* stupid."

"What?" Ivy exclaimed. "I invite you into my camp and all you do is insult me. I want you to leave this instant."

Fargo did not budge. "All I meant was that you must have a real good reason for setting yourself up as a walking target for every curly wolf between here and the border."

"The best of reasons," Ivy said angrily. "Mr. Stockwell is paying me four hundred dollars. It might not sound like much money to a famous scout like you, but to me, it's more than I can earn in a year of waiting on tables or washing dishes."

"Is the money worth your life?"

Bristling, Ivy rose onto her knees. "Who the hell are you to judge me? You're a *man*. If you were a woman, you wouldn't be so high and mighty. You would know how hard it is to make ends meet." She clenched her fists until her knuckles shone white. "All the lousy jobs that no one else will do! All the jobs that don't pay half as much as most men make! And when a woman does land one of those jobs, what happens? She's still paid less than men. It isn't fair."

Fargo had struck a raw nerve without meaning to. He would be the first to admit that women on the frontier had it hard, but so did the men. Cowpunching, mining, prospecting, they were all grueling, dangerous work. "I'm sorry," he said.

Ivy blinked. "You are?"

"I would hate to see anything happen to you, is all. You're too nice a person to end up with a slug in your back courtesy of a money-hungry weasel."

The compliment did not have the effect Fargo imagined. Thunder crackled on Ivy's brow and she stabbed a finger at him. "You don't fool me, mister. For all your fine talk, I know what you're after. The same thing all men are after." Flouncing upright, she stormed off into the night.

Fargo began to rise, to go after her, but he changed his mind. Maybe it was best if she had some time to herself. Whatever was eating at her was something she had to work out herself.

Taking his coffeepot, he walked to the stream and filled it. In due course the fragrant aroma of brewing grounds filled the crisp air. He munched on a cracker, then cleaned the Henry to kill time. He was pouring his first cup when Ivy came out of the woods and took a seat without comment. Hefting the pot, he said, "Would you like some?"

"Please," Ivy said. It was as if the argument had never occurred. She did not refer to it again, and neither did he.

Leaning back, Fargo sighed in contentment. "City dwellers are always asking me why I like to live in the wilderness. They always want to know what the mountains and the desert have to offer that a city doesn't." He nodded at the myriad of stars sparkling on high. "They wouldn't need to ask if they saw that."

Ivy gazed heavenward. "I never figured you for the type to notice."

"Why? Because I'm a man?"

"No. Well, yes. I would be lying if I didn't admit that I think most men tote their brains below their belts. Tom Grifter never once admired the stars. And my pa was always too busy working or whatever to see the beauty in nature."

Fargo liked how the firelight played on her skin. "I see the beauty," he said, and was rewarded with a blush.

Sipping her coffee, Ivy made herself comfortable. "You vex me, Skye Fargo. You vex me like no man ever has."

"That's only because you've never roped one and put your brand on him," Fargo guessed.

Ivy snickered. "Shows how much you know, Trailsman. I was married once." She laughed when Fargo betrayed his surprise, but the laugh was as cold as ice and as flinty as quartz. "That's right. Me. The man-hater. I had me a husband and all the trimmings that go with being a wife. A little cabin. A flower patch. A dog and a cat and a goat that ate our clothes when I hung them on the line to dry."

Fargo did not know what to say so he said nothing. Unwittingly, he had opened a breach in the damn that pent up her innermost thoughts and feelings.

"It was nice, at first. My pa didn't bother me anymore. And my husband tried his best to make ends meet. We talked of having a real house one day, of raising a passel of kids." Ivy brightened. "Those three months were the only happy ones of my whole life."

Fargo could not believe that. She had to be in her early twenties. Surely her childhood had been fairly pleasant. But what was that she had said about her father bothering her?

"Then my husband lost his job. He was caught drinking. And like he always did when he got upset, he drank more. And more. Until he turned ugly and nasty and did things he shouldn't ought to have done."

Gone was the smile. Torment marred her features, torment that worsened as she went along. "I tried my best. I reasoned with him. I pleaded with him. I begged him. Got down on my knees and *begged* him. But he wouldn't mend his ways. He took to staying out late with his old friends. He'd come home so drunk he could barely stand, reeking of liquor. And when I complained, he—"

Ivy stopped, chalk white, gasping. Raising a hand to her chest, she sucked in a long breath to calm herself. "Now it's me who is sorry. I shouldn't burden you with my woes. What is done, is done. Water under the bridge, as they say."

"Some scars take a long time to heal," Fargo remarked.

"Isn't that the truth."

Their eyes met, and for a few fleeting seconds they shared a bond of understanding that bordered on outright tenderness. Then the moment was gone, shattered by a loud *snap* from the fire and a spray of sparks. She swatted them aside, nervously chuckled, and sat back to finish her coffee.

Little else was said until they turned in. Fargo lay listening to her heavy breathing, flattered that she trusted him enough to fall asleep before he did.

The next morning Fargo was up at first light. He had rekindled the fire and was heating what was left of their coffee when Ivy stirred and then sat up.

"Goodness. I slept like a baby. Haven't done that in weeks."

"You're safe so long as you're with me."

Ivy did not take offense. "Yes, I'm beginning to see that I am. I just hope you don't turn out to be another crummy back stabber." Popping out from under her blankets, she stretched, unaware that her shirt had shifted while she slept and now hung low over her shoulder.

Fargo could not avoid seeing the swell of her breast. She was right there in front of him. And she caught him staring. He braced for an outburst, but to his amazement she calmly adjusted the garment, picked up her gunbelt, and walked off toward the stream without so much as a sour glance. Just the day before she would have put a slug into him.

"Women," Fargo muttered. While she prettied herself up, he treated himself to black coffee strong enough to dissolve nails. He passed on eating food. The jostling his stomach was soon to endure was best endured empty.

His hunch proved correct. Ivy was in a hurry to make up lost ground. She held the dun to a trot more often than not, and did not stop to rest until the sun was directly above them. By then they were over the Divide and paralleling the Mora River on its generally southeasterly course.

In a shaded glade they halted. Ivy removed her boots and dipped her feet in the cool water, saying, "Some folks claim it's their legs or their backsides that get sore after a lot of time in the saddle. Me, it's my feet. Why do you reckon that is?"

Fargo was sure he had no idea.

Ivy arched an eyebrow at him. "By the way. You haven't mentioned where you're bound?"

"Sumner's Trading Post."

"What a marvelous coincidence," Ivy said dryly. "That's exactly where I'm going." She pursed those ruby lips. "Thinking of entering the Great Footrace, are you?"

"Not hardly," Fargo said. "Tell me about it, though."

"There's not much to tell. The starting gun is fired at seven in the morning on the tenth, rain or shine. The course is twenty-five miles long—"

"Twenty-five *miles*?" Fargo interrupted. The longest footrace he had ever witnessed covered only a mile. "They must not want anyone left alive to reach the finish line."

Ivy chuckled. "In previous years most of the runners have been Apaches and Pimas and whatnot. Very few whites entered. This year promises to be a lot different."

Fargo pondered. The hefty grand prize would lure people out of the woodwork to take part. But the Indians would have a decided edge. Especially the Apaches. From an early age, Apache boys were trained to run incredibly long distances without food or water or rest. By adulthood, the average warrior could cover seventy-five miles in a single day. Hard to believe, but true.

"I might even enter my own self," Ivy mentioned.

"You?"

"Why not? When I was a girl growing up on the farm, I learned to run faster and farther than any of the other girls, and most of the boys besides."

The region in which the trading post was located was mostly desert. Fargo had been through it a couple of times before. Twenty-five miles in that sweltering heat would wither most runners like grapes drying on a vine. He told her as much.

"That's why so few ever make it all the way to the end," Ivy said. "But I haven't told you the best part. The course runs south along the Pecos River. All that water, and not a drop to drink."

"Why not? The Pecos isn't tainted."

"Anyone who gives in and takes so much as a sip from the river is out of the race. They post men all along the course to make sure no one cheats."

Apaches could go that long without water, but Fargo knew of few others who could. He doubted that even he could do it, and he'd had plenty of practice going for lengthy spells without a drink. "I'm glad I'm not taking part," he said.

Presently they were under way again, Ivy in the lead. The dun was tired but game and Ivy maintained a brisk pace until late in the afternoon.

"We won't reach Fort Union by dark," Fargo brought up.

"So we'll spend another night under the stars," Ivy said. "What's wrong with that?"

Fargo was going to tell her nothing was wrong when he was distracted by a jay that abruptly took noisy wing a few hundred feet ahead and to the left, from the slope of a ridge that overlooked the Mora River. Whatever had spooked the bird did not appear. An animal of some kind, he figured, and gave it no more thought.

Ahead the river bubbled around a bend. Leafy trees grew

in profusion, restricting Fargo's view of whatever was beyond. Suddenly a buck and a doe flashed from the trees, crossed the trail, and plunged into vegetation on the other side.

Ivy tried to unsling her rifle but the deer were gone in a twinkling. "Darn," she said. "I wouldn't mind a thick venison steak for supper tonight."

"What about the rest of the animal?" Fargo said. "Or do you plan to spend a whole day drying the meat over a rack?"

Ivy scrunched up her mouth. "I see your point. Oh, well. Once Mr. Stockwell pays me, I'll have enough money to treat myself to restaurant cooking. Maybe I'll go to Santa Fe and eat at the Benedict House. It's the finest in the whole territory."

"I'm surprised the marshal didn't post you out of town the last time you were there."

"What do you—?" Ivy said, and blushed. "Oh. You heard about Spencer, the drunk I had to shoot."

"Had to?"

"What would you do if a man grabbed you as you were walking by an alley and forced you up against a wall at knifepoint? He groped me, and boasted as how he was fixing to do me right, as he put it." The memory soured Ivy's mood. "When he went to undo his pants, I got a hand free. His mistake."

Attempted rape. Fargo couldn't blame her. "Better hope you never run into him again. A man like that is liable to hold a grudge."

"Spencer? He's too yellow to give me any more trouble. I taught him a lesson he'll never forget."

They were rounding the bend. Fargo was almost abreast of the dun and focused on Ivy, not the trail. So he was as startled as she was when someone cackled with sinister mirth.

"Is that a fact, sister? I must be a slow learner, 'cause here I am, loaded for bear. Or should I say, loaded for a bitch?"

Three mounted men barred the way. All three were cut from the same ruthless cloth as Hardwick had been. All three wore vicious smiles. And all three had shotguns pointed at Fargo and Ivy Cambridge.

5

Shotgun. The very word sent shivers down the spines of saloon rowdies. No one in his right mind would buck a lawman holding one. A shotgun loaded with buckshot was a handheld cannon. While a rifle had more raw knockdown power, and a pistol could be brought into play faster, a scattergun could practically blow a man in half.

So when Skye Fargo found himself staring down the muzzles of three of them, he made no move toward his Colt or the Henry. It annoyed him that he had let the men take him by surprise. He should have been more alert, more observant.

The coyote named Spencer was enjoying himself. Wagging his weapon at Ivy Cambridge, he sneered, "What's the matter, woman? Cat got your tongue?"

A broad-shouldered man with a scruffy beard, on Spencer's left, laughed. "She looks like she swallowed a walnut without cracking the shell."

"At her age, Jeeter, she ought to know that life is plumb full of surprises," Spencer said.

"And some of 'em are nasty," said the third rider, the runt of the litter. At some point in the past his nose had been broken and never set properly. It bent sharply in the middle, making his whole face appear lopsided.

Spencer nudged his mount a few feet closer. "Did you really think I'd forget what you did to me, Cambridge?"

Ivy found her voice. "You brought it on yourself. You tried to tear my clothes off."

"I was drunk!" Spencer responded. "I didn't know what in the hell I was doing. And you damn near ruined me for life." Glancing at his groin, he shuddered. "For two months I was laid up in bed. For two months I couldn't heed Nature's call without the pain reminding me of you."

"Do you want me to say I'm sorry?" Ivy said. "Well, I won't. A woman has the right to defend herself from men who take undue liberties."

Spencer swapped amused looks with his companions. "Listen to her. Can she really be this stupid?" Leaning forward, he told her, "You could apologize until doomsday and it wouldn't change a thing. I'm not about to forgive and forget. I'm not no Bible thumper."

"Maybe you should forgive her," Jeeter said with a wink. "Maybe the two of you should kiss and make up. And after you're done, Foster and me will kiss and make up to her, too."

All three men laughed.

Fargo had been largely forgotten. Jeeter's shotgun was trained on his chest, but Jeeter had not bothered to cock it yet. Moving slower than thick molasses, Fargo crept his right hand toward his pistol.

Spencer was savoring the moment. "Do you have any idea of the humiliation you put me through? How many jokes were told at my expense? How men would laugh behind my back? How people pointed me out on the street and whispered to their friends?"

"You should be thankful you're alive," Ivy said lamely.

"Oh, I'm thankful, all right," Spencer said. " 'Cause now I get to give you a taste of your own medicine. Now I get to watch you grovel and groan and bleed all over yourself."

Foster stared at Ivy's saddlebags. "The money first. Don't forget the money."

Spencer nodded. "How can I forget? That's what gave me this brainstorm." He kneed his horse even nearer. "You see, I heard all about how you'd be taking the prize money from Taos to Sumner's Trading Post. That feller Stockwell came to Santa Fe a couple of weeks ago and crowed to everybody who would listen."

Twice now, Stockwell's loose lips had put Ivy in jeopardy. Fargo could not help but wonder if the newsman planned it to happen, if maybe Stockwell hoped to spice up his account of the Great Footrace for his readers.

"I got to thinking," Spencer had gone on, "how I could kill two birds with one stone. Steal me a heap of money and pay you back, all at the same time."

"How did you know I'd be coming this way?" Ivy said. "I never told anyone the route I would take."

"Oh, that was easy as sin. Horses need water, don't they? And once over the Divide, the Mora here is the only water to be had for miles around. I figured you'd follow it to Fort Union, then head south to the trading post."

Jeeter shifted in the saddle. "Can't we get this over with before winter sets in? I want to get back to Taos and drink myself under the table to celebrate my windfall."

"Not me," Spencer said. "After I'm done with her, I'm heading for St. Louis, or maybe New Orleans. I'm going to buy me clean clothes and sleep in a fancy hotel with a four-poster bed and have fillies in skimpy outfits wait on me hand and foot."

Foster snorted. "Why go that far to see a pretty face? Me, I'm going to go through the local girls, alphabetical-like. I'll start with the A's and work my way down to the Z's, and if I got enough money left, I'll go through them again."

"Ain't he a hoot?" Jeeter said, chuckling.

"A real caution," Spencer agreed, then turned grimly serious. "All right, bitch. Climb down."

Ivy did not budge. "I can't let you have the prize money. It's not mine."

"What difference does that make?" Spencer retorted. "In a little bit, it'll be ours. Now get off, or so help me I'll blow you out of that saddle." To emphasize the threat, he pointed the shotgun at her head and cocked one of the triggers.

Jeeter and Foster were glued to Ivy in anticipation of seeing her head explode like a pumpkin. Fargo's right hand was between his belt buckle and his holster, still not close enough. He snaked it to the right, prepared to draw if it appeared that Spencer would actually fire.

"I ain't got all day," the vengeful curly wolf snarled.

Ivy rested a hand on her saddle horn and began to dismount. "You'll never get away with this. Mr. Stockwell will have you hunted down and hung. Just you wait."

"That dandy?" Spencer said. "What makes you think he cares what happens to you? All he's interested in is adding readers to his paper. If you and the money disappear, he'll just hire another fool female to make the run."

One foot out of a stirrup and about to slide down, Ivy paused. "You're forgetting the law."

"I haven't forgotten anything. We're out in the middle of nowhere. The only lawman who has jurisdiction is the federal marshal, and he's so overworked he can't afford to spend more than a few days trying to figure out what became of you." Spencer clucked in triumph. "I've got it all worked out, woman. I'm even going to have word spread around that you stole the money yourself, then lit out for California."

"No one who knows me would ever believe such a bald-faced lie."

"You'd be surprised what folks will believe," Spencer said. His tone hardened. "Quit stalling. Do as I told you, and move away from your animal."

Fargo watched Ivy obey. His hand was a couple of

inches from his pistol. A quick flick of his wrist was all it would take. It would be best, though, if the three gunmen were not paying any attention to him, and Jeeter picked that moment to say, "What about this feller, Spencer? Do we turn him into worm food, too?"

Spencer glanced at Fargo. "I don't know who you are, mister. But you're sure in the wrong place at the wrong time. We can't leave any witnesses."

"Give me five hundred dollars and my lips are sealed," Fargo said.

"What?" Ivy declared, her hurt transparent. "You were after the money all along?" Her jaw quivered and she took a step, body arched to hurl herself at him. "I should have known. You men are all alike! Not one can be trusted."

Spencer grinned from ear to ear. "You're after the same thing we are?" he said to Fargo. "Well, that's interesting. What do you say, boys? Do we cut this jasper in?"

Jeeter was quick to answer. "Not on your way. I've got my heart set on a full share."

Foster took longer but his decision was the same. "We don't know this guy from Adam, Spencer. What's to keep him from taking the money and turning us in later on?" Foster shook his head. "Besides, I don't like the way he looks. He reminds me of a bobcat I caught once as a kid. Even caged, I knew that if I stuck my hand in, it would bite off a finger."

"I guess that's that," Spencer said, smirking at Fargo. "Sorry, mister. But if it will make you feel any better, you don't need to worry about that stallion of yours. I promise to take good care of it."

Jeeter leveled his scattergun, his thumb on the left hammer. "Let's get this over with."

Fargo desperately needed a distraction. Even if he shot Jeeter, at that range one of the others was bound to cut him down. He pressed his legs against the Ovaro to lever himself from the saddle.

Then the underbrush crackled, and a distraction was provided, but from a most unlikely source. A small doe, a timid straggler, pranced out of the trees and up the slope after the deer who had fled earlier. She was gone in four bounds, passing behind the mounts of the three would-be robbers.

Spencer and his partners did what most anyone else would have done. At the crackle of the brush, they glanced over their shoulders, Jeeter going so far as to swing his shotgun partway around.

Fargo's right arm blurred. He had the Colt up and out before any of them realized he had gone for his gun. His first shot punched Jeeter backward. His second caught Spencer high in the shoulder. As he swiveled to shoot Foster, the runt leaned low over the far side of his horse.

Spencer, swaying, his shirt stained scarlet, brought up his gun. His hands were wildly unsteady, and it was that, more than anything else, that saved Fargo's life. For in the brief moments it took Spencer to hold the shotgun level, Ivy Cambridge produced her Smith & Wesson. She fired just as Spencer was about to, fired again as he reeled. Gamely, Spencer tried to train the shotgun on her, but at a third shot a new nostril blossomed and he toppled, the scattergun clattering to the ground beside him.

Jeeter had straightened. Foam flecking his lips, he lifted his weapon.

Fargo fanned the Colt, two swift blasts that flung Jeeter earthward in a disjointed pile. The drumming of hooves signaled Foster's escape. Fargo wheeled the pinto, but Ivy's dun was between them and the skittish horse reared.

Ivy spun, tracking Foster, holding the Smith & Wesson in a two-handed grip. He was riding Comanche style, only his forearm and the lower third of his leg visible. She snapped off a shot and his elbow dissolved in a spray of bone and crimson. Yelping, Foster fell. His horse kept on going. He landed on his shoulder and instantly rolled to his knees. His left arm was useless but he brought up the shot-gun with his right.

Fargo and Ivy fired a heartbeat apart. Twin slugs cored Foster's head, jerking it backward. Mouth agape, he sprawled to the earth. The shotgun discharged into the ground, spewing dirt and grass over a wide area.

Ivy spun again, toward Fargo. The Smith & Wesson's hammer clicked loudly. For a few unnerving seconds he honestly thought she was going to shoot. "I wasn't serious about wanting a share," he said softly.

"Do you expect me to take your word for it?"

Paying her no heed, Fargo dismounted. He verified Jeeter and Spencer were dead. To reach Foster he had to pass Ivy, and she had still not lowered her pistol. "If you're going to put lead into me, then do it," he rasped.

"I should," Ivy said, gnawing her lip. Suddenly hissing, she snapped the revolver down. "But I can't," she lamented. "I can't shoot someone in coldblood."

Fargo had no need to bend over Foster. The man's brains were oozing out. "We'll take the bodies with us and hand them over to the officer in charge at Fort Union. He'll get word to the federal marshal."

"Why bother?" Ivy said. "I'd as soon let the buzzards eat them."

"It's better if word gets around," Fargo said. "It might keep others who have the same notion from trying to steal the prize money."

"I reckon it would at that," Ivy reluctantly conceded.

And those were the last words she spoke until well after sunset. They set up camp in a hollow where their fire could not be seen from afar. Fargo killed a rabbit and butchered it. Ivy prepared coffee.

Now and again Fargo made comments to entice her into conversation, but she would not rise to the bait. She turned in early, her back to him, her blanket pulled up over her head.

Next morning, the sun rose cheery and warm, but the same could not be said of Ivy. She growled at Fargo when he said "Good morning." It was downhill from there.

Fargo led Jeeter's and Foster's animals, Ivy handled Spencer's. The shotguns were bundled in Fargo's bedroll for safe keeping. Uneventful hours of steady travel brought them within sight of the next outpost of civilization.

Fort Union had been built on the Mountain Branch of the Santa Fe Trail, near Wolf Creek, a tributary of the Mora River. Since it served as a supply depot for all military posts in the region, as well as a deterrent to the Jicarilla Apaches, it was one of the largest in the territory. Not only did it boast comfortable living quarters, as forts went it had a hospital, an ordnance depot, a quartermaster's store, and a commissary, a laundry, and a *bakery*. Mule skinners would travel a hundred miles out of their way just for a taste of the bakery's various sweet pastries.

Arriving at the fort with three bodies in tow created quite a stir. A sergeant materialized almost immediately, listened to Ivy relate her account of the gunfight, and promptly ushered them to headquarters.

Colonel Edward Canby was cordial and outspoken. Standing in front of the three mounts laden with their stiff burdens, he said, "I'll inform the marshal that in my opinion the killings were justified. It's a clear case of self-defense." He looked at Ivy and scowled. "But none of these men would have lost their lives, young lady, if you weren't party to Stockwell's harebrained venture."

"You wouldn't say that if you knew him. He's a fine person—for a man," Ivy said.

"But I *do* know him," Colonel Canby said. "He's been through here half a dozen times since this whole nonsense began." The officer's scowl deepened. "This is strictly off the record, you understand, but if Frank Stockwell has a shred of genuine character in his body, he keeps it well hidden."

"Keep your opinions to yourself, if you don't mind," Ivy said stiffly. Unwrapping her reins from the hitching post, she said, "I'm going to water and rest my horse. In two hours I'll be out of your hair, Colonel. Good day."

Canby stared after her. "Hardheaded, isn't she? Is the lady a friend of yours, Mr. Fargo?"

"More or less."

"I'd watch out for her, were I you."

Fargo aimed to do just that. Touching his hatbrim, he ambled a dozen yards in her wake. Over by the corral a smith was repairing a busted wagon wheel. Five supply wagons were lined up, ready to depart once the wheel was fixed. The drivers lounged nearby.

Ivy was halfway to the stables when a bewhiskered specimen leaning against the rails let out with a whoop and a holler and dashed toward her, his arms outflung. "As I live and breathe! Ivy! Give this ol' coon your paw, child!"

Cambridge stopped dead. "Benjamin? Is that you?" Aglow with happiness, she embraced him heartily, saying, "It's been so long! I feared you had gone to your reward!"

"I'm too ornery for the devil to want me," the old-timer said, his cheeks moistening. He was as lanky as a broom handle, his Spartan frame covered by buckskins that had seen better days before Ivy was born. His hair and beard were the color of fresh driven snow.

Unnoticed, Fargo halted. He had wanted to talk to Ivy, but now it could wait.

"Let me take a gander at you, girl," Benjamin said, holding her at arm's length. "You look healthy enough, but there's a sadness to your eyes. What's the matter? Is that no-account pesterin' you again?"

"I'm fine," Ivy said.

"Sure you are," the mule skinner said. Scanning the parade grounds, he huffed. "Where is the varmint? I'll skin 'im alive if he's causin' you grief."

Fargo had never seen Ivy Cambridge so happy. But it was short-lived. Tenderly brushing the old man's cheek with her fingers, she sagged against him and said softly, "Benjamin, Benjamin, Benjamin."

"Nice to know you ain't forgot. I've been meanin' to look you up, but I'm haulin' freight for the blamed army now, and they keep me pretty busy."

Ivy straightened and squeezed his hand. "Tell you what. I need to see to my horse, but in about half an hour why don't we meet at the bakery and I'll treat you to those sugar-coated sinkers you like?"

Benjamin gave a spry hop. "You're on, girlie! And I'll buy the coffee!"

Fargo had not made it a point to eavesdrop. He was so close, he could not avoid overhearing. As Ivy moved on, so did he, but his way was unexpectedly barred by one hundred and fifty pounds of human rawhide.

"Big ears can be cut off," the mule skinner said, his left hand resting on the well-worn hilt of a bowie. "Maybe you should explain your interest in my little girl, friend." He held up his hand when Fargo opened his mouth. "Before you say it's none of my damn business, keep in mind that she's the closest thing to the daughter I always wished I had. I'm only lookin' out for her welfare."

"That makes two of us," Fargo said, and introduced himself. "I ran into her north of Cantonment Burgwin." Briefly, he related the incident with Tom Grifter and the encounter with Spencer.

"That was you and her who brung in those bodies?" Benjamin said. "I was over to the depot, but a pard told me about it." Eyes as gray as morning mist raked Fargo from hat to spurs. "She's lucky you were along. But tell me plain. Are you fixin' to break her heart like all the other men in her life?"

"I'm not out to marry her, if that's what you're hinting," Fargo replied. "She could use a friend. It's as simple as that."

Benjamin turned to regard Ivy's retreating figure. "Truer words were never spoke. That poor gal has had more than her share of heartache." He tugged at his beard. "Know her story, do you?"

"No. She's as tight-lipped as she is sassy."

Chuckling, Benjamin gestured for Fargo to accompany him to a corner of the corral. As they walked, he said, "You can't blame her for being so feisty once you've heard her tale. I came across her in a tiny armpit of a town in west Texas. She was penniless and scrawny from lack of food. Reminded me of a lost puppy."

"Was this after her folks died?"

"Died?" Benjamin stopped short. "That what she told you? Hell, son. They're still alive. More's the pity."

"Why?"

"Her pa. The things that brute did to her—" Benjamin flushed and grit his teeth. It was a minute before he could continue. "One night she had too much wine and broke down and told me the whole story. How her pa beat her with a rod nearly every damn day."

"The scars," Fargo said to himself.

Benjamin looked up. "You know about 'em? That's just

part of it. If I was to tell you the whole tale, your blood would curdle."

"So that's why she hates men."

The mule skinner leaned against a rail. "That's not the half of it. I got her back on her feet and found her a decent job. She was startin' to act human again, when along came that sweet-talkin' polecat who swept her off her feet. I tried to make her see he was worthless, but she was blinded by his hot lips. She had to have him. And they got hitched."

"She told me a little about it."

"Did she tell you how after she said "I do," that bastard treated her like she was his personal property? He slapped her around all the time, called her names when she didn't fetch his food fast enough to suit him or cook it just the way he liked. When he was drunk, which was just about every other day, he beat her black and blue. And abused her in other ways."

Fargo was gaining whole new insights into why Ivy Cambridge despised men. And he couldn't say he blamed her.

"Finally she came to her senses and cut out. She wanted a divorce but the scoundrel won't agree to one, so she's stuck being his wife. On paper at least."

"Maybe someone will do her a favor and bed him down permanently."

"I wish you had."

"How's that?"

Benjamin's brows knot. "You said she told you, so I took it for granted that you knew. Guess I was wrong."

"About what?"

"Her husband. You had a chance to set her free and you blew it." Benjamin paused. "It's Tom Grifter."

6

The freight wagons were not the only ones at Fort Union. Shortly after arriving, Skye Fargo had noticed a mud wagon parked near the laundry. He did not think much of it at the time.

Daily, travelers stopped at the post. With only a few restrictions, they were allowed to make use of the facilities as they pleased so long as they did not interfere with the regular military routine.

But after Benjamin left to meet Ivy, Fargo strolled around the parade ground to stretch his legs. He turned between the two barracks, passed the hospital and the sutler's, and was close to the mud wagon when a high-pitched squeal of delight rang out.

"Skye Fargo! Don't you dare move a muscle, you big, adorable bear of a man!"

Fargo turned and was nearly bowled over by a runaway steam engine. Only this train was two-legged and shaped like an hourglass. It had on a bright green dress decorated with ribbons and bows and lacy frills. And a sweet fragrance clung to it like a cloud. Slender arms embraced him. Warm lips found his cheek. Girlish giggles tinkled in his ear.

"How have you been, lover? I haven't seen hide nor hair of you since Kansas City. Remember?"

Fargo untangled himself and got a good look at the vivacious creature beside him. Gorgeous brown hair that cascaded past bare shoulders. A creamy complexion and rosy lips lent added appeal. Playful brown eyes sparkled with zest and humor.

"Clara Gilliam," Fargo said. Fond memories washed over him, memories of three wild nights in Denver spent in the dove's stimulating company, of a whole week later on in Kansas City, a week of drinking and dining and making love each and every night until they were exhausted. She was one of the few women who could hold her own against him, drink for drink, tit for tat. Her appetite for sensual pleasures rivaled his own.

"What in the world are you doing in this godforsaken neck of the woods?" Clara inquired.

"I could ask you the same question." As Fargo recollected, Clara was very selective about the men she "entertained." Luxury hotels and the finest of restaurants were her usual stomping grounds.

"Oh, four of us working girls came to this awful place on a lark, and I can't tell you how sorry I am," Clara explained. "It's all Stockwell's fault. The cheap bastard."

"You know Frank Stockwell?" Fargo said, surprised. "Tell me all about it."

Clara entwined an arm in his. "Not out here in this hot sun, handsome. Let me invite you into my parlor." Tittering, she hustled him toward a row of small cabins situated apart from the rest of the post's facilities. "The guest quarters, the army calls them. Fit for a queen, that colonel told me." Clara snorted. "Fit for roaches and mice is more like it."

Fargo had to agree that army accommodations left a bit to be desired. But the cabins were furnished with a bed and dresser and a small writing table, and they were spotlessly clean. "I don't see where you have much to complain about," he remarked.

Clara pushed him into the chair, then perched on the

edge of the bed. "Of course you'd say that. You sleep on the ground most of the time and think it's heavenly, for God's sake. But I like silk sheets and quilt covers and breakfast in bed." She sniffed in distaste. "Stockwell promised us that we'd travel in style and stay at the best places money could buy. Stupid me. I forgot that in New Mexico, there's nothing worth buying."

Despite himself, Fargo laughed. "Tell me about Stockwell," he repeated.

"Why are you so interested?" Clara said. "Don't tell me you're involved with that stupid Great Footrace of his?"

"No. But I have a friend who is."

Clara's delicate eyebrows arced. "This friend wouldn't happen to wear skirts, would she?" Grinning impishly, Clara rose and sashayed to the chair. Brazenly, she deposited herself in his lap, facing him. "I might know a thing or two about Franky that you'd find of interest. But the information will cost you."

Fargo glanced at the closed door, then at the partly drawn curtains. "Let me guess," he said.

"One good turn deserves another," Clara said, leaning forward until her bosom brushed his chest. Her forearms rested on his broad shoulders, her warm breath found his face. "And I'm so bored and lonely, I could cry."

"You? Lonely? In a fort full of soldiers?"

"The boys in blue are off-limits to us working girls. Colonel Canby made that abundantly clear." Clara pouted, her red lips forming a delicious oval. "We've been stuck in this hole for three days. Our mud wagon broke down. Something to do with the axle. And it can't be fixed until a part is sent from Taos."

"Poor baby," Fargo quipped.

Her pout deepened. "You can be cruel, you know that?" She tossed her hair over a shoulder and lightly ran a long fingernail from below her jaw to the border of her dress, deliberately dallying at the swell of her breasts. "I'll forgive you if you'll relieve the boredom."

Fargo's manhood twitched. He would like nothing better than to frolic under the covers, but Ivy Cambridge was leaving in half an hour or so. "I don't have much time—" he began.

"So we'll make it quick," Clara said and boldly lowered her lips to his.

The warmth, the softness, the enticing taste of her silken tongue kindled a familiar hunger. Fargo cupped her chin and she cupped his, her fingers running through his beard. When she eventually broke for air, they both breathed heavily.

Clara's eyes were hooded, her voice husky. "Mmmmm, that was nice. Just like I remembered. You're about the best kisser alive. When you die, they should bronze your lips."

Fargo laughed again. For the first time in days he was fully relaxed, feeling carefree. Clara always had that effect on him. It was another reason he was so fond of her. "The notions you have," he said.

"I'm having another," Clara teased. "Had it the second I laid eyes on you out there." The tip of her tongue rimmed her mouth invitingly. "I haven't been with a man for over a week and I've got the hunger, bad."

The scent of her perfume was overpowering, the warmth of her lush body stimulating beyond words. Fargo felt his mouth go dry. He stared at the expanse of bare flesh jutting from her bodice and a lump formed in his throat.

"Come on. For old time's sake," Clara said. She kissed his forehead, his left cheek, his right cheek. She nibbled on his jaw, tiny light kisses that could drive a man insane. The whole while her hands roamed over his back and down around to his legs. Knowing fingers stroked his inner thighs.

By the time Clara got around to locking mouths again,

Fargo could not have stopped if the cabin was on fire. Her hunger fueled his own. His manhood leaped to attention, and his hands covered her bodice, massaging the globes underneath. A low moan escaped her. She pressed against him, her hips grinding in a slow rhythm.

As Fargo's need mounted, so did the urgency. He snatched at the ribbons and bows, undoing her dress enough for his right hand to slip underneath and cup a taut breast. A hard nipple mashed against his palm. She quivered when he tweaked it, gasping in abandon.

"Ohhhhh, I knew this would be fun. Wait. Let me give you a hand."

Pulling back, Clara wriggled and tugged, shrugging the dress down to her slim waist. She started to pry at her underthings, but Fargo was not inclined to wait. Gripping the fabric, he wrenched. Clasps popped. Buttons flew. A rip appeared. Clara slapped his hand, declaring, "You brute! Now look at what you've done! And I can't sew a lick."

Fargo's mouth swooped to an upcurved breast. Greedily, he sucked on the nipple, swirling it around and around with his tongue. Clara inhaled loudly. Pressing both hands against the back of his head, she ground his face into her chest. In the process his hat fell off.

"Ummmmmm. Keep it up, big man."

Switching to the other breast, Fargo gave it the same treatment. He cupped the undersides of each, caressing them, the friction warming her skin and adding to the sensations his mouth provoked.

Always a talker, Clara cooed, "You sure do know how to stroke a girl's flames, Skye. I'm burning up down below."

Fargo had to see for himself. His right hand dived under her dress and probed upward. Contacting glass-smooth skin, he traced a path to her velvet inner thigh. Her legs trembled as he slowly climbed higher, drawing out the suspense for all it was worth. He could feel the heat long before he touched her. Clara's womanhood was an inferno of rampant desire. His forefinger dipped and brushed her nether lips. She was dripping wet, and at his touch she threw back her head, bending her spine into a bow.

"Ahhhhh. Put it in! Put it in!"

Fargo obliged. Her sheath closed around his finger, clinging to it, molding like a glove. At his first stroke, Clara clamped her teeth on his shoulder and bit down, hard. Her fingers raked his back. If not for his buckskin shirt, her nails would have ripped him raw.

Fargo's thumb discovered her knob. Rubbing it, he elicited a strangled cry. It occurred to him that anyone passing by outside would overhear, but he did not stop. He didn't care. All that mattered was the moment and the willing woman in his arms.

"The bed," Clara husked.

Wrapping his arms around her waist, Fargo rose. She accommodated him by forking her willowy legs around his hips. Locked in intimate embrace, they reached the bed and fell, Clara on the bottom.

Heated kisses were exchanged. Fargo's right hand delved into her depths, his left switched from one heaving mound to the other. For her part, Clara explored every nook and cranny on his body. When she lowered a hand between his legs and cupped his organ, he feared that he would explode then and there.

Exercising self-control, Fargo commenced pumping his finger in and out. She clung to him, her head tossing, her creamy face framed by a halo of rich hair. A glazed look of utter carnal hunger came over her and she mewed again and again like a little kitten. Her left hand yanked his shirt free and slid up under it.

Fargo winced when her nails drew blood. Clara had always been a hellion in bed. Any man who bedded her bore the marks for days.

"Oh, I want it so much!"

The feeling was mutual. Fargo bunched her dress around her midsection, exposing her legs. She bucked against him to spur him on, her lower mount rubbing his rigid pole. The pleasure it brought him was exquisite. In return, he added a second finger in her tunnel and twirled both around and around.

Clara gushed. Grasping his shoulders, she heaved and spurted and thrust against his hand as if to impale herself. "More, more, more!" she cried.

Fargo did not need much encouragement. Unhitching his pants, he let them slide to his knees. Positioning himself, he placed the tip of his manhood at the entrance to her core, then paused.

"Sadist!" Clara exclaimed. "What are you waiting for?" She clawed his back, his ribs, his hips. She kissed him, bit him, lathered the crook of his neck with her tongue. And when she was pulsing with need, when she was twisting and thrashing and as hot as a furnace, Fargo gave her what she wanted.

In one powerful stroke, Fargo buried himself to the hilt. For a few moments Clara lay still, lost in sublime ecstasy. A short thrust galvanized her into hurling her body upward as if striving to send them both flying through the roof. Her legs clamped around him in a vise. She glued her lips to his, her tongue in constant motion.

The need for release built in Fargo, starting at the base of his spine and slowly working its way upward. Holding her hips, he stroked evenly, smoothly, driving so deep into her that he lifted her off the bed. Her ardor equaled his. She matched his passion, kiss for kiss, feel for feel, thrust for thrust.

"Oh! Oh! Oh!" Clara cried, and erupted a second time. She was a wildcat and a volcano and a flood, all rolled into one. She swept him to the pinnacle. She crested at the brink and carried him along with her.

Her release triggered his. Fargo wanted to hold off awhile longer but his body would not be denied. His manhood throbbed, and the next moment he was over the summit and soaring, soaring, soaring, his senses in a whirl. It seemed to go on forever and ever. Gradually, he became aware of his surroundings. His breathing slowed. He coasted to a stop and lay panting on top of Clara, who wore a supremely satisfied smile.

"Thanks, handsome. I needed that."

Fargo pecked her breast. She wasn't the only one. For five minutes they were still, relishing the peace, the solitude. He broke the spell by rolling off and propping his head in his hand. "You promised to tell me about Stockwell."

Clara cracked an eye. "My, my. Aren't you the persistent one?" Sighing, she snagged a pillow and raised her head to lie on it. "Very well. What do you want to know?"

"Everything."

"Let's see. He showed up at Fanny's Sporting Palace about a month ago. I didn't cotton to him much, but the other girls sure did. To hear the man crow about himself, you'd think he was God's gift to the world."

"One of those," Fargo said.

Nodding, Clara elaborated. "He went on and on about how he had cooked up this scheme that would make him rich and famous. Mostly rich. He was on his way back to New Mexico, and he convinced some of the girls to tag along. It would be a grand adventure, he claimed. Told us that we could pick up a lot of money working the crowds he's expecting to be on hand for his silly race."

"I'm surprised you agreed."

"What can I say?" Clara responded. "We were half drunk at the time. And Mabel, my best friend, insisted that both of us should go. It would be fun, she said." Clara swore.

"Mabel always was a few marbles short of a bag, if you know what I mean."

Fargo sat up. "Is Stockwell here at the fort?"

"No. The rat bailed out on us. He couldn't wait for the mud wagon to be fixed, so he went on ahead. We're to meet him at Sumner's Trading Post. For two bits, though, I'd turn around and go back to Kansas City."

Hiking his pants, Fargo buckled the belt.

"Why are you so curious about Franky?" Clara asked, and went on before he could answer. "Be careful if you tangle with him, lover. He's a rat, but a rat with claws. One of the girls told me that he carries a derringer up his right sleeve and a dirk up his left."

"Most newspaper reporters settle for a pencil and pad."

"If he's a legitimate reporter, I'm the Queen of England. I swear, that man could talk a virgin out of her chastity. He has a gift for gab like few men I've ever come across. Word is, he was involved in some shady dealings in New York City and Philadelphia and nearly got run out of town on a rail."

"What newspaper does he work for?"

"Strange thing, there," Clara said. "He's told everybody that he works for a big eastern paper, but no one can peg him down as to which one."

"It shouldn't be hard to find out," Fargo said. "I heard that the paper put up the seven thousand dollars for the prize money."

Clara snickered and crooked a finger to draw him closer. "That's what everyone thinks. But Mabel told me that Stockwell connived a bunch of businessmen into putting up the pot."

"You believe her?"

"Why would she lie? Besides, Mabel got it straight from the horse's mouth, lover. Stockwell spent four or five nights with her and blabbed more than he should."

"What do the businessmen hope to get out of it?"

"Advertising. Tons of it, Stockwell promised them. Businesses from Sante Fe to Kansas bought into the brainstorm." Clara covered her breasts and began adjusting her clothes. "Like I said a minute ago, that devil could talk rings around a tree."

Fargo wondered how much, if any, Ivy Cambridge knew. Probably none of it, or she wouldn't believe that Frank Stockwell walked on water. "Heard anything about the courier he hired to deliver the seven thousand?"

"Not much," Clara said. "A country hick who is putting her neck on the chopping block for peanuts." She smoothed her hair. "I'd hate to be in her shoes. Every money-hungry vulture in these parts will be after that poke."

Fargo swiftly finished dressing. After strapping on his gunbelt, he retrieved his hat and stepped to the door. "I'll look for you at Sumner's Trading Post."

"Can't you stay a little longer?" Clara asked wistfully. "As I recall, you get your second wind faster than any galoot on either side of the Mississippi." She winked mischievously. "I'm ready for a second helping if you are."

"Any other time," Fargo said sincerely. Going to the bed, he gave her a last kiss, then had to pry her hands off to leave. Her throaty purr followed him outside.

"I'll hold you to that! Sumner's it is! And you won't get away so easy down there."

The shadows were longer than Fargo expected. The dalliance had delayed him an hour and a half, judging by the sun. He made straight for the Ovaro, noting along the way that the freight wagons were gone. The mule skinners had already pulled out.

With a sinking feeling in his gut, Fargo climbed on the stallion and rode to the dragoon stable. A private was sweeping it out. "Has Ivy Cambridge been by to claim her dun?"

"That pretty blond lady, you mean? Yes, sir." The soldier fished out a pocket watch which chimed when he opened it. "Almost an hour ago, it's been. Lit out of here like the wind, she did."

So did Fargo. Mentally kicking himself for his lapse in judgment, he sped southward. Eventually he would strike the Pecos River. Once he did, reaching Sumner's was a simple matter of following the Pecos to the southeast.

Surmounting an hour's lead would take skillful riding. Fargo had gone over five miles before he struck Ivy's trail, and right away he saw that something was wrong. Overlapping the dun's tracks were those of another horse. Someone was shadowing her. It could only mean one thing.

Throwing caution to the wind, Fargo drove the stallion at a breakneck pace. He figured to overhaul the pair by nightfall. If not, he would press on. Ivy's life was forfeit if he failed her again.

It soon became apparent that Cambridge had not held to a straight course. Again and again she doubled back to check her back trail, but she only looped around for short distances. And whoever was hunting her was shrewd enough to stay far, far back. She never spotted him.

The heat climbed as the afternoon lengthened. It was hard to believe it was only May. Fargo would have sworn the month was July or August.

Fifteen miles from Fort Union, in a wash shaded by a sawtooth ridge, Ivy had stopped. The prints showed where she had roosted under a tree while the dun grazed on a meager patch of dry grass. From where she sat, she could see for a mile or more along her back trail. Evidently she suspected that she was being followed but once again the rider dogging her tracks eluded detection.

The Ovaro needed rest but Fargo trotted on. Every minute wasted was crucial. Whoever was after the money would not wait long to make his bid. Certainly no longer than nightfall, when Ivy would make camp and be a sitting target for any skulker in the brush.

Sunset was less than thirty minutes off when Fargo climbed to the top of a hill and saw, in the distance, the silhouette of a man on horseback. The range was too great to note any details, and no sooner did Fargo set eyes on the rider than the man went over a rise and was gone.

It gave Fargo the incentive to spur the pinto with renewed vigor, but try as he might, the sun surrendered the sky to the stars and still Fargo had not overtaken him.

To the southeast a firefly glowed. Ivy's campfire, Fargo guessed. Out in the open where it should not be. Hinting that she felt confident no one was after her. She was in for a rude surprise unless Fargo beat the would-be robber at his own game.

Chaparral provided enough cover for Fargo to approach without being seen. Two hundred yards from the fire, he drew rein, ground-hitched the stallion, and advanced on foot, the Colt in hand.

A convenient arroyo gave him a means of sneaking to within a hundred feet or so of Ivy's camp. Crouching, Fargo cat-footed along the bottom. In near-total darkness he wound around the many twists and turns. When he judged that he was near enough to the site, he slowed. The walls were fairly steep, but at one point the slope was slanted enough for him to climb it upright.

Fargo glided toward the rim. He heard the dun nicker and paused to determine which direction the wind was blowing. It would defeat his purpose if the horse caught his scent and its whinnies sent Ivy into the dark to investigate. She was the bait for the trap he wanted to spring.

A crunch of gravel turned Fargo to the left just as an inky form hurtled over the side of the arroyo—toward him.

7

Skye Fargo whipped his Colt up and out but he was not quite fast enough. The hurtling figure slammed into him and they tumbled. Steel glinted dully in the starlight. Fargo snagged a wrist, stopping the big knife an inch from his heart. They rolled to the bottom, winding up on their sides in a swirl of dust.

His attacker was as wiry as a panther. Kicking, the man planted his foot in Fargo's stomach and wrenched to free his arm, but Fargo held on and slashed the Colt's barrel at the man's temple. It struck a glancing blow.

For an instant his attacker weakened. Fargo lunged, throwing himself astride the man's chest and raising the revolver on high to deliver a blow that would end the fight. Just then, the arroyo flooded with light. A pistol discharged, the slug thudding into the dirt next to Fargo's leg.

"Stop it! Both of you!"

Fargo glanced up. Ivy Cambridge held a firebrand in one hand, her Smith & Wesson in the other.

"I mean it! Get off of him, Skye! He's like a second father to me."

Looking down, Fargo realized that the man he had been battling was none other than Benjamin. The muleskinner acted just as surprised. "You!" both of them blurted at the same moment.

Fargo lowered his arm and rose. "Sorry, old-timer," he said. "I thought you were a thief after the prize money." Offering his hand, he helped Benjamin to stand.

The muleskinner chuckled. "And I thought you were Grifter or one of his no-account pards. I've been followin' Ivy without her knowin', watchin' her back." Benjamin slid his bowie into its sheath. "Since the two of you didn't leave the fort together, I figured you had gone your separate ways. I reckon the joke's on me, eh?"

Fargo did not share in the mule skinner's laughter. They were extremely lucky that neither of them had been hurt. The mistake could have cost one of them his life. "Weren't you supposed to head out with those freight wagons?"

Benjamin nodded. "Another driver took my place. I got the colonel to give me some time off. Canby ain't such a bad sort. And he was eager to help out, since it was for little sister's sake."

Above them, Ivy Cambridge cleared her throat. "Am I supposed to be grateful? Am I supposed to be pleased by the fact that both of you obviously think I am not able to take care of myself? Should I jump for joy that you treat me as if I'm a ten-year-old girl instead of a grown woman?" Replacing the Smith & Wesson, she stomped off, plunging the arroyo into darkness.

"What in the world brought that on?" Benjamin said. "All we're tryin' to do is see that she gets to Sumner's safe and sound."

"See you in a bit," Fargo said, and headed up the arroyo to fetch the Ovaro. Personally, he was glad the muleskinner was along. Two men could protect Ivy better than one. It took some of the burden off him.

Loud voices rose from the clearing as Fargo led the stallion into it. He had arrived in the middle of a heated dispute. Benjamin was wagging a finger at Ivy and being as stern as any natural father would.

"Don't you take that tone with me, Missy! Maybe I was a mite sneaky. But I only had your best interests at heart." He moved between the fire and where she sat on a flat boulder, but she would not meet his gaze. "Seems to me, you should be glad instead of mad."

"I resent being treated like a child."

"Then quit actin' like one! We both know that your mangy husband won't stop tryin' to get his hands on that seven thousand. If not for Fargo, he'd already have it, and you would be pushin' up daisies come spring."

"I won't make the same mistake twice. I'm more careful now."

Fargo broke in. "You call this being careful?" He gestured at the fire. "Making camp right out in the open?"

Ivy's glare would have withered a flower. "I did it on purpose. I had a notion that someone was behind me, and I wanted to lure him in. So I set a little trap." She pointed at her bedding, which she had cleverly arranged to give the impression she was asleep under the blankets. "How was I to know that it was only you two idiots."

"Idiots!" Benjamin declared. "Is that the thanks I get for frettin' myself silly? Is that what you call someone whose only sin is he cares for you?"

Ivy fidgeted. "Don't twist things around. I'm not the one who should feel guilty."

Benjamin dropped onto a knee and clasped one of her hands. "Child, at least you're alive *to* feel. And I want to keep you that way. If I did wrong in sneakin' along to protect you, I'm sorry. But I'd do it again in a second if I had to. You mean more to me than anything."

The frank declaration left Ivy speechless. She went to say something but had to cough. Her eyes misting, she hugged the muleskinner close and said softly, "I'm sorry, Benjamin. I shouldn't pick on you. You've never done me wrong."

"And I never will, missy."

Fargo stripped the pinto and spread out his bedroll. His rumbling stomach reminded him that he had gone all day without a bite to eat. At the sutler's he had bought some jerky, so he helped himself to a piece.

Ivy was staring at him. "I reckon that I shouldn't be put out at you, either. It must have taken a lot of willpower to tear yourself away from your lady friend."

Fargo stopped chewing in the middle of a bite. "Who?"

"I didn't learn her name," Ivy said, bending to the coffeepot. "I went hunting for you before I left the post. Just to say *adios,* you understand. A soldier told me that he'd seen you with one of those fancy ladies who were staying at the fort. He pointed her cabin out. But when I got close, I could tell that the two of you didn't want to be disturbed. All those creaking bedsprings, and that caterwauling."

It took a lot to embarrass Fargo. He could not remember the last time it had happened, or the last time he had blushed. But he felt his cheeks growing warm now, and he said, "She's an old friend of mine."

"A real *close* friend, no doubt," Ivy said casually.

Too casually. Was it Fargo's imagination, or was Ivy upset by his fling with Clara? "Not all women are manhaters. Some like being with us as much as we like being with them."

"I can't imagine what they see in any of you. Except for Benjamin, none of you are worth the bother it would be to blow every last mule-headed male to kingdom come."

The mule skinner guffawed. "Why, thank you, child. But thank goodness most female critters don't think as you do, or the human race would come to a mighty quick end." Playfully nudging her, he added, "Besides, a few bad apples don't spoil the whole basket. Sooner or later a young feller is going to come along who will treat you decent. Then you'll see things differently."

"Maybe," was all the further Ivy would commit herself. To change the subject, she said, "I plan to reach the trading post by the day after tomorrow, so I'm getting an early start. Be up and ready or I'll leave you behind."

Benjamin sighed. "Still a mite prickly, I see. What did you do? Sit on a cactus earlier?"

Ivy chose not to reply. Little else was said, and presently Benjamin and Ivy turned in. Fargo was not all that tired, so he sat up late, keeping guard. The stars were uncommonly bright, the night serene. Toward midnight, he had the feeling that he was being watched, and gazing across the fire, he saw the flames reflected in Ivy's wide open eyes. "Can't you sleep?" he asked.

Sitting up, the blonde ran a hand through her golden hair. "I've dozed a few times, but I always wake up again. Just restless, is all. I guess this business is getting to me."

"It would get to anyone," Fargo said. He liked how her hair shimmered, and the rosy sheen to her skin. She was a beauty, this woman. It was too bad that life had treated her so cruelly. She deserved better.

Ivy idly traced a pattern in the dirt. "What was your friend's name?" she asked out of the blue.

Puzzled, Fargo told her, adding, "Clara and I have known each other a few years. The last I knew, she was in Kansas City."

"She sure sounded like she was enjoying herself."

There it was. Out in the open. "I'd like to think she did," Fargo admitted.

"She must like you an awful lot. I mean, you meet up, and right away you go off by yourselves and . . . well, you know."

"Clara likes *men* a lot." Fargo kept the news about Stockwell to himself. For one thing, Ivy would not believe him. For another, he had to learn how much she knew before he confided in her. He doubted she was a party to whatever Stockwell was up to, but he had to be sure.

"Oh. One of those," Ivy said. "I never have understood women like her. How can they let men touch them for money? How can they stand all that abuse?" She paused. "Have you two ever fought?"

"No."

"You've never hit her, not once? Never slapped her around to keep her in line?"

"Why would I do that? Clara's free to live as she damn well pleases." Fargo decided to cut right to the quick. "Most men aren't like Tom Grifter. Or like your father."

Ivy stopped doodling. "Where did you hear about him?" she demanded. Then, glancing at Benjamin, she answered her own question. "Darn. I should have guessed. I saw the two of you talking by the corral. What else did he tell you?"

"Not much," Fargo said. "But enough to show that he loves you."

"Sweet Benjamin," Ivy said tenderly. "He doesn't have a bad bone in his body. He's always so kind, so considerate. I shudder to think what might have happened to me if he hadn't come along when he did."

"There you have it."

"Have what?"

"The proof you needed that not all men are heartless bastards. You made a mistake with Grifter, but the next time will be better."

"I wish I had your confidence." Ivy chewed on her lower lip until the distant yip of a coyote sparked her to ask, "What about you, Skye Fargo? Any notions of having a wife and family? Of maybe putting down roots?"

Men like Tom Grifter would have lied. They would have told her what they felt she wanted to hear just to win her over. Fargo told the truth. "No. There's a lot of this country

I haven't seen yet." Her disappointment was as plain as the frown that curled her full lips. "I was bitten by the wanderlust bug when I was knee-high to a buffalo calf," he explained. "I always have to see what's over the next horizon."

"And the ladies you spend time with, ladies like Clara, they don't mind?"

"Why should they? Just because two people take a shine to each other doesn't mean they're meant to spend the rest of their lives together. I imagine that Clara will find herself a beau one day and settle down to what most folks call a proper life. Most like her do."

Ivy stared at him again, stared so long and so hard that Fargo grew vaguely uncomfortable. "Something the matter?"

"No. Yes. I don't rightly know." Ivy shook her head, then closed her eyes. "You do things to me, Skye Fargo. I don't mind admitting that. And you scare me, scare me more than anyone I've ever met. You make me think that there's a better life just waiting for me, if only I'll reach out and grab hold of it."

"What's wrong with that?"

"Nothing, I reckon. But I've been so used to being miserable that I'm afraid of being happy." Ivy's forehead furrowed. "Isn't that strange? Why should that be? You'd think it would be the other way around." Sighing, she stretched out. "My head hurts from all this thinking. Good night, Skye. Sorry to bother you."

"It's no bother." Fargo poured a cup of coffee and stayed up for another half an hour, sipping and pondering. Soon Ivy would make up her mind. Then what? Should he politely decline?

Fargo had to smile. Certain friends of his would laugh themselves silly at the thought of him turning a willing young beauty down. But he had never taken advantage of a woman, never manipulated one, never resorted to tricks and lies to get what he wanted. For all his faults—and he would be the first to admit that he had more than a few—he took pride in always being honest, in always doing what he felt was right.

So what if he liked to drink now and then? So what if he enjoyed a friendly game of cards? So what if he was partial to the company of pretty females in lace and lavender? He was a *man,* for God's sake. He would offer no apologies for doing what came naturally.

Soon he turned in, his last sight the rhythmic rise and fall of Ivy's ample bosom.

The next morning they were under way before sunrise. Through the predawn gray they trotted to the southeast, riding in single file with Fargo in the lead. Few words were spoken. They were in the heart of Apache country. Diligence was called for. For although a tenuous truce was in effect, many an unwary traveler had lost his belongings and his life to roving bands of young warriors eager to prove themselves in the time-honored Apache ways.

To steal without being caught. To kill without being slain. Those were the Apache mottos. Before the coming of the white man, the various Apache tribes had raided and pillaged to their heart's content. From Sonora and Chihuahua in Mexico, from Texas to the east and Arizona to the west, the Apaches had been lords of their vast domain.

Repeated skirmishes had taught the Apaches that resisting the whites in force was too costly. Largely thanks to the efforts of Cochise, their revered leader, the Apaches no longer waged constant war. But it would not take much to set them off. Both sides distrusted the other. Many whites hated Apaches simply because they were Indians; many Apaches hated the whites simply because they *were* white. New Mexico was a powder keg waiting for the right spark to explode.

Whoever came up with the idea of the annual race at Sumner's Trading Post was playing with fire. So long as it was conducted fairly, there would be no problem. But let an Apache be cheated just once, and there would be hell to pay.

Such musings occupied Fargo most of the morning. Several times he caught Ivy studying him on the sly, but he never made mention of it. During their midday rest, she went off by herself. When she came back, she had undergone a surprising change.

Ivy had swapped her baggy pants for a tighter pair. In place of her baggy shirt she wore one that she apparently reserved for special occasions, a garment that bore out her womanly assets to a striking degree. Her floppy hat went into her bedroll so her luxurious mane could hang loose and full. "My everyday clothes were getting grungy," she said to explain the change.

Benjamin pretended to scratch his beard, his hand covering his mouth. But he could not hide the crinkles at the corners of his eyes.

Before long they reached the Pecos River. On the east side was the trail to Sumner's, rutted by wagon wheels, the earth churned by countless hooves. Fargo saw that seven or eight riders had passed that way within the past few hours. White men, since the horses had all been shod.

"I sure do love the wilderness," Benjamin remarked, inhaling deeply. "If I wasn't so powerful fond of mule skinning, I'd most like to be a mountain man. Livin' wild and free is how we were meant to be."

Fargo agreed wholeheartedly. He was going to say as much, but the crack of a rifle from half a mile or so ahead put an end to small talk. Reining up, he listened for more shots. None rang out.

"A hunter, maybe?" Benjamin said.

Fargo did not think so, not unless it was a hunter with bronzed skin, knee-high moccasins, and a headband. "I'll take a look. The two of you stay here until I get back."

Ivy goaded the dun up next to the Ovaro. "Why only you? What if you run into trouble? We're tagging along."

To refuse would get her dander up. Fargo spurred the pinto into the growth bordering the sluggish Pecos, yanked the Henry out, and levered a round into the chamber. Pausing often, he covered more than half a mile without finding any spoor. Then the stallion bobbed its head and shied from a dark spot on the right.

It was a pool of blood.

Fargo climbed down to examine the ground. Boot prints and shod hoofprints told the story. A pair of white men had shot a deer, loaded it onto a spare horse, and ridden southward at a leisurely gait. Swinging into the saddle, he tracked them for fifteen minutes, to the mouth of a narrow canyon.

"They might be prospectors," Benjamin guessed without much conviction. "There are a lot of gold-hungry old coots wanderin' these parts."

"We'll know soon enough," Fargo said, veering toward a slope that would take them to the north rim. The climb was precarious. Loose stones and dirt cascaded from under their animals, and near the top it became so slippery they had to dismount and guide their horses on foot.

Muffled voices warned them that they were close. Leaving their mounts, they stalked along the rim until fingers of flame gave away the location of the camp. Ducking low, Fargo padded to a cluster of boulders that overlooked the canyon floor. Screened from view, he peered down.

Six men ringed the fire. Another two were carving up a dead doe. Their horses were picketed in a string between the men and the canyon wall. Revolvers and rifles were much in evidence.

"Well, well, well," Benjamin said bitterly. "Look who it is."

Prominent among the gunmen was Tom Grifter, Zeke at

his elbow. Somewhere or other Grifter had collected six more of his violent breed, men who lived by the gun and the blade, men who held no compunctions about killing when it suited their purpose, or when the pay was right.

"They're after the money," Ivy said coldly. "They must think I'm ahead of them somewhere, and they're hurrying to catch up."

Were they? Fargo wondered. Based on the tracks he had seen along the Pecos that afternoon, the killers were in no great hurry. They had even stopped early for the night.

Benjamin leaned a shoulder against a giant boulder. "I wish I was Samson so I could shove these over the edge. We'd settle Mr. Tom Grifter's hash once and for all."

Fargo had a better idea. The badmen had picked an ideal spot to camp in that no one could get near them from either end of the canyon without being seen. But with a little ingenuity, he could overcome that problem. "Benjamin, bring all three of our ropes," he whispered.

The muleskinner scampered off without asking why Fargo wanted them. Fargo searched for a boulder no higher than his chest but wide enough and heavy enough to support his weight. He found one that would suffice. Roving his hands over it, he confirmed there were no sharp edges. The crunch of loose earth let him know Ivy was right behind him.

"You're loco if you're planning to do what I think you are."

"We need to slow them down. If you can think of a better way, I'm all ears." Fargo waited, and when she did not respond he handed her the Henry, then sat to remove his spurs. "It's the one thing they won't expect."

"Of course not. No one would be crazy enough to try a stunt like this. Don't do it. I won't have your death on my conscience."

Fargo flashed a grin. "Why, Ivy, I didn't know you cared."

"It wouldn't be right, is all," Ivy said, flustered. "Don't go putting words in my mouth. We're friends, nothing more. I still hate men just as much as I ever did."

She was not being honest with herself or with him but Fargo did not rub her nose in it. "Just promise me that no matter what happens, you won't take up with Frank Stockwell. He's no better than Grifter. Maybe a lot worse."

"How can you accuse the man when you've never met him?" Ivy countered. "You should hear about the time he raised money to help poor people in New York City, or the time he saved a little girl and her puppy from a raging flood in Pennsylvania." She started to raise her voice but realized her mistake and snapped quietly, "You should be half the man he is, Trailsman."

Fargo was saved from having to comment by the arrival of the mule skinner, who dumped the coiled ropes at his feet. Tying the ends together, Fargo tested the knots by having Benjamin pull on one rope while he pulled on the other. Fashioning a wide noose, he wormed it around the boulder he had selected until it was nice and snug.

"I trust you'll wait until they're asleep," Benjamin said.

"It will be too quiet. They're liable to hear me." Fargo moved to the edge, his back to the cliff. "Just be ready to haul me up when the time comes."

"And how will we know when that is?" Ivy asked.

"When all hell breaks loose." Making a loop around his waist, Fargo held the rope securely, braced his feet, and slid over the edge.

8

Seventy feet. Not far at all. Or so Skye Fargo tried to convince himself as he carefully worked his way down the rope. He tried not to dwell on the fact that at any moment the strands might snap, or his hand could slip. He tried not to think of the gruesome result should he plummet to the jagged boulders scattered below.

None of the killers looked up. The pair carving the deer were bent over the animal, their long knives slicing and slashing. As for the rest, they were joking and laughing and having a grand old time. Making enough noise, Fargo hoped, to keep them from hearing the faint sounds he made.

The movement of the rope worried him. Since it was not anchored at the bottom, the lower third wriggled and swayed like a snake with every movement he made. Should any of Tom Grifter's band gaze toward the cliff, they were bound to notice.

Most of the horses were dozing. A sorrel near the end pricked its ears when Fargo's boot scraped against the wall, but it relaxed after a bit, head drooping.

Lowering one hand at a time, his boots clamped together with the rope between them to better support his weight, Fargo went steadily lower. Cigar and cigarette smoke tingled his nose. He could also smell coffee, the fresh scent of blood, and the odor of horse droppings.

The voices became clearer. A wiry hardcase in the clothes of a cowhand, including chaps, was speaking in a bearish growl. "—got to hand it to you, Grifter. This scheme of yours is the most clever I ever heard of. No one will suspect you were the brains behind it."

Tom Grifter smirked. "I can't claim all the credit, boys. Don't forget the *hombre* who came up with the idea for the Great Footrace in the first place. He's the real brains."

"He's a jackass," disagreed another man, a tall drink of water packing two pistols. "A dude who is so in love with himself he should walk around with a mirror strapped to his chest."

Zeke glanced up. "That's silly. Why on earth would a grown man want to do that?"

"So he can admire himself every chance he gets," the man answered.

Tickled, Zeke laughed, a few of the others joining in. "That's a good one, Boothe."

"Too bad that female has such a big lead on us," commented the cowboy. "It would save us a heap of trouble."

"Not as much as you seem to think, Pardee," Grifter said. "We'd still need to wait until we had it all. Timing is everything." He scanned the circle of hard faces. "Be patient. Do as I say. And this will work out just fine."

What was Grifter referring to? Fargo wondered, and paid for his lapse in concentration when his sweaty left hand slipped. He started to fall. Thrusting upward, he snagged the rope again, but it cost him a patch of skin. His palm was scraped raw before he brought himself to a stop.

Blood pounding, Fargo clung there a few seconds, calming himself. That had been close. He must focus on what he was doing, and nothing else. Nothing whatsoever.

Zeke had found a twig and stuck it into a corner of his mouth. "I like your idea, Tom," he told his cousin, "but I ain't partial to hurtin' Ivy. I don't like that one bit."

"It can't be helped," Grifter said. "She's bound to figure out I was to blame and set the law on our trail. Do you want to spend the rest of your days on the dodge?"

"No," Zeke admitted. "But I'm right fond of her, Tom. She's always treated me decent. Treated you decent, too, as I recollect. What you have in mind ain't right. No, sir."

Pardee and several of the others were rankled by Zeke's attitude, and the cowboy was quick to say, "What *I* don't like is how you're always griping about taking care of the woman. You're too pussy-kitten for my liking."

"That's right," said another, placing a hand on a revolver. "How do we know you won't turn soft on us and warn her? How do we know you won't spoil the whole thing?"

"Anyone who turns on us won't live long enough to brag about it," warned a third.

Tom Grifter angrily smacked his leg, getting their attention. "Enough! I won't abide such talk. Zeke is kin to me, in case some of you didn't know. Anyone who lifts a finger against him answers to me. Savvy?"

Sullen nods and curt replies only angered Grifter more. "I mean it." He put a hand on Zeke's shoulder. "Sure, he's a jackass. Sure, he's given us a hard time about this." He put a hand on Zeke's shoulder. "First he griped because we're tryin' to steal the money for ourselves instead of makin' sure it gets to Sumner's like the boss wants. Now this." Grifter clapped Zeke on the back. "A regular worrier, that's my cousin."

"If you say so," Pardee said.

"Look," Grifter declared, "if Zeke ruins this for us, I'll settle with him personally. You have my word."

A bearded man grunted. "That's good enough for me, Tom. You've never gone back on a promise before."

By this time Fargo was halfway down. His left palm stung terribly but he ignored the discomfort. He froze when he saw that one of the horses was staring at him. When it did not betray any alarm, he eased lower.

Zeke was chewing on the twig. "That's not true," he said to the bearded hardcase. "Tom went back on his word once."

Grifter tensed. "What are you talkin' about? When did I ever fail to keep a promise?"

"You broke the one you made to Ivy, remember? You vowed to love, honor, and respect her. Those were the preacher's own words. Yet you didn't. You beat on her and called her nasty names and—"

Tom Grifter smacked Zeke. "Son of a bitch!" he snarled. "You have a lot of gall. I just stuck up for you, and you do this?"

"All I meant—" Zeke began.

"I know damn well what you meant." Grifter would not let his cousin get in a word edgewise. "I should gut you here and now for the insult." Grabbing the front of Zeke's shirt, Grifter shook him. "Haven't I looked after you since your folks were massacred by those filthy Injuns? Haven't I always made sure you had clothes on your back and food in your belly? You stinkin' half-wit! If it wasn't for me, you'd be rottin' in some jail by now, or six feet under."

Zeke tried to peel his cousin's fingers off but couldn't. "Please, Tom. You're scarin' me."

"I hope to hell I am!" Grifter thundered. "Maybe it will teach you to keep your mouth shut from now on." Incensed, he shoved, spilling Zeke on his back. Some of the others chuckled, their mirth cut short when Grifter rose and spun, his hand clawed near his revolver. "Which one of you thinks this is so damn funny?"

No one answered.

Grifter kicked Zeke's leg. "Don't you ever mention Ivy again? You hear me? Not so long as you live."

Zeke did not know when to leave well enough alone. "But she was always so nice—"

"To *you*!" Grifter exploded. "But you weren't married to her. You didn't have to put up with her naggin' and carpin', day after day after day. Nothin' I ever did was good enough to suit her."

"All women are like that," Pardee mentioned. "Bitching is in their blood, I reckon."

"That's the gospel," Boothe said. "I was married once. The woman about drove me mad, always saying how I didn't earn enough money and how we should have a bigger house and more clothes and whatnot. There was no pleasing her."

Grifter pointed at the two men. "There? You hear that, Zeke? It wasn't all my fault. Ivy brought a lot of it down on her own head."

By now Fargo was within eight feet of the ground. He dipped lower still, then froze when one of the men butchering the deer rose and came toward him carrying the animal's severed head.

"Don't want to keep this around to draw flies," the man idly said. Almost to the shadows, he flung the head to the earth, wiped his bloody hands on his pants, and went back.

Fargo was amazed the man had not spotted him. The head was less than a yard away. He hurried even lower, and the next moment his feet touched solid ground.

A sullen silence had descended on the camp. Zeke had sat up and moved away from his cousin, who was glaring at everyone and anyone. The tension was broken when the two men who had carved the doe brought a haunch to the fire.

"Who's hungry, boys?" one asked.

By unanimous agreement, they were all starved. As Fargo moved along the wall, talk and gruff laughter broke out again. The cutthroats were excited by the prospect of getting their hands on the prize money.

Crouching, Fargo slid his Arkansas toothpick from the slender sheath strapped to his right ankle. The double-edged blade was honed to razor sharpness. So the first rope he applied it to parted with no problem. One by one he went down the line and cut loose each animal. The horses looked at him, unsure of what he was up to, but none whinnied or stomped or pulled away. Done, he crouched and retraced his steps. It had gone easier than he thought it would.

At that juncture, Boothe rose and came toward the string. "I'll fetch my 'bacca," he said over a shoulder.

Several saddles and saddlebags had been draped over a long, low boulder. Going to one of the latter, he opened it and rummaged inside. Producing a leather bag, he was rising when one of the horses nickered softly.

Fargo was in indigo shadow at the base of the cliff. He pressed against it as Boothe studied the string, then advanced cautiously. Did the man suspect? Fargo held the toothpick against this thigh, ready to bury it between Boothe's ribs if the man came too close.

The hardcase halted. Something was bothering him about the horses, but he could not seem to put his finger on exactly what. He patted the hindquarters of the mount that had nickered.

For anxious seconds Fargo worried that the animal would step backward or swivel to either side, which would show that its tether had been cut. But the horse stood there. Boothe, with a shrug, pivoted and rejoined his friends, handing the tobacco to Pardee.

Fargo replaced the toothpick and hastened to the rope. Gripping it, he gave a little hop and climbed hand over hand, his legs dangling.

"What's that?" a gunman asked loudly, and rose to his feet. "I heard something."

Had it been the rope swishing against the wall? Fargo stopped, six feet up, as the gang scoured the canyon from end to end. Two of the men looked right at him but did not detect him in the gloom.

"You're hearin' things, Kline," Grifter said. "There's no one else within fifty miles of us."

"Except for Apaches," Kline said. "A band of Mescaleros was seen in these parts a week ago. They say it was Cuchillo Negro's bunch."

Black Knife. Fargo had heard the name before. Cuchillo Negro was a renegade who hated outsiders and had launched a hopeless campaign to drive all whites from Apache lands, just as his grandfather had done against the Spanish and his father against the Mexicans. It was claimed that Cuchillo Negro was without mercy. No atrocity was too vile. He had vowed that no whites would be spared. Not the men, not the women, not even children.

"That's saloon talk," Grifter said. "Cuchillo Negro has been operatin' west of here for over a year. Everyone knows it."

"I'm only telling you what I heard," Kline said, reluctantly sitting back down.

Fargo's shoulders were growing sore. His arms ached. He had to reach the top swiftly, before he tired, but he dared not move while the killers were alert and watchful. Suddenly, to the east, a rock clattered noisily. Every last hardcase sprang to his feet and whirled, pistols glinting in the firelight.

Fargo was as startled as they were. Could it be that hostile Apaches were abroad? Grifter and the rest fanned out and headed up the canyon. Immediately, Fargo pumped his arms, scaling the rope as fast as he could, his shoulders growing worse with every yard gained. Three quarters of the way up, he happened to glance at the fire and was stunned to see Zeke still seated on a boulder and *staring up at him.*

The Trailsman stopped. It was impossible to say whether Zeke had seen him or not. Zeke's expression gave no clue. Yet if Zeke had, why didn't he shout to alert the others? Fargo waited thirty seconds, then climbed on. His arms were about ready to give out when his right wrist was gripped from above and he was hauled onto the rim.

"Damn, you had me worried," Ivy Cambridge whispered. "I thought for sure they would spot you."

"They heard something," Fargo said.

Ivy smiled impishly and hefted a small stone. "I know. I was going to throw another if they headed back before you reached us."

Benjamin knelt beside them. "I ain't seen her fret so since the time I gave her a kitten for a weddin' gift and one mornin' it disappeared. Likely a coyote got the poor critter." Grasping the rope, he began pulling it up. "Let's get this over with before those vermin catch on."

Fargo unfastened the rope from the boulder. Coiling it over his shoulder, he stepped to the edge. Zeke had not moved. The others were a hundred yards or so away, searching. Taking the Henry, he aimed at a point between the horse string and the wall. "Here goes," he said.

At the initial blast, most of the horses shied and pranced. Screeching like an Apache, Fargo levered more rounds into the canyon. Benjamin added high-pitched yips, while Ivy hollered lustily. The combination was enough to spook the animals into panicked flight. Breaking to the right and the left, they swept around the fire, a few passing within an arm's length of Zeke, who made no attempt to catch them.

Shouts and curses resounded up the canyon. Shots rang out, until Grifter bellowed, "Stop firin', you fools! You'll hit our horses!"

Fargo jogged to the Ovaro and mounted. By the time he

reached the canyon mouth, the fleeing horses were nowhere to be seen.

"We did it." Benjamin chuckled. "It'll take those varmints a month of Sundays to round up their nags."

"We'll reach Sumner's with no problem now," Ivy said.

Would they? Fargo questioned. Other badmen were bound to be after the money. And if Kline was right about a war party being in the area, every white in the territory was in danger. He would not rest easy until they arrived at their destination.

Two and a half days later, they did.

It was early afternoon when Fargo rose in the stirrups and spied the woodland in which the post had been built. Called the Bosque Redondo, or the Round Woods, the trees formed a belt sixteen miles long and half a mile wide, at the widest. They were by no means thick, but there was enough wood to meet the needs of the man who ran the trading post, Niles Kendall.

Duly licensed back in '51, Sumner's had been named in honor of Lieutenant Colonel Edwin Vos Sumner, whose California Column of Dragoons had been largely responsible for quelling an uprising. It was a lonely outpost in the heart of the wilderness, one hundred and twenty miles from the nearest military installation. But the Apaches and the Navajos had never attacked it.

Part of the reason was that Kendall always treated the Indians fairly. He did not sell liquor and would not allow others to do so; he reported whiskey runners to the army. During a particularly fierce winter a few years back, he had won the lasting gratitude of the Apaches by taking blankets and food to them when they were in dire need, at his own expense.

Sumner's Trading Post was neutral territory, a place where whites and red warriors put aside their hatreds, at least temporarily, for the sake of the common good. Troublemakers knew they would be kicked out, or shot.

Fargo had been to the post a couple of times before. Never during the annual footrace, though. So he was mildly shocked to find hundreds of Indians present, Apaches and Navajos and Pimas and Maricopas in separate camps, while around the walls of the post itself had sprung up a tent city sprinkled with lean-tos and a crude log cabin or two.

"Tarnation!" Benjamin exclaimed. "I didn't expect so many. It's worse than Denver."

The muleskinner was exaggerating, but he had a point. It was a simmering cauldron of humanity that might boil over if tempers were to flare. Fargo kneed the Ovaro down the rise. To reach the post, he had to pass between the camps of the Apaches and the Pimas. Long bitter enemies, the two tribes were as different as night from day. The Apaches lived by their wits, raiding and plundering, while the Pimas were peaceful farmers who had befriended the whites—and earned undying Apache hatred for doing so.

Warriors from both camps warily eyed Fargo and his friends. The Apaches wore headbands and long-sleeved shirts and high moccasins unique to their kind. The Pima men were bare-chested, or favored colorful blankets draped over their shoulders. Pimas never cut their hair, which hung in wide plaits down to the calves of their legs.

Fargo could feel the tension in the air. The right provocation, and Sumner's Trading Post would become a battleground. He saw a swarthy Apache studying Ivy intently and hoped it did not bode ill. Numerous times in the past, Apaches had stolen women they took a shine to, whites and Mexicans alike. The women of Sonora and Chihuahua so feared being taken that when Apaches were reported in their vicinity, they locked themselves indoors and would not venture out until assured the raiders were gone.

A row of wagons sat outside the trading post, near a tent

much larger than any of the others. From it wafted tinny piano music and the off-key singing of a woman whose voice cracked on the high notes. Coins tinkled. A pair of females in tight dresses stood at the flap, beckoning passers-by.

"Lordy," Benjamin said. "Doves and gamblin'. Now all we need is liquor, and we might as well start diggin' graves."

As if to prove his point, a pair of young Apaches wandered past, walking unsteadily. Fargo frowned. Someone was selling whiskey. And the Indians did not call it fire-water for nothing.

The trading post gates hung open. Inside, bedlam reigned. People bustled to and fro. The store was thronged with Indians and whites alike. So many horses were tied to the hitching posts that Fargo could not find a spot for the Ovaro. Riding to a corner of the building, he swung down and looped the reins around the jutting end of a log.

"It's a madhouse," Benjamin said. "Are all these folks here for the stupid race?"

"Appears so," Ivy said. "This is nothing like last year. Only a couple of hundred were here then, and most of them were Indians. Now there must be pretty near a thousand, over half white."

Fargo followed her in. To say the place was doing brisk business would be putting it mildly. The aisles were jammed, the counters packed. Half a dozen clerks were not enough to deal with the constant demand for service. "By the time this is over, Niles Kendall will be a rich man," he remarked.

"Money isn't everything, friend," said someone to their left. "Not if it costs lives."

Niles Kendall was partially screened by some dry goods. Offering his hand to Fargo, he shook warmly. "It's been a while, Trailsman. Don't tell me that you're here for the race? I credited you with more commonsense."

"I came with Miss Cambridge," Fargo explained, stepping aside when a pair of Navajo children darted down the aisle, the oldest trying to snatch a sweet from the youngest. "I didn't count on this."

"That makes two of us," Kendall said. He was a portly man, his store-bought clothes neat and clean. A big Walker Colt rested in a holster on his left hip, butt forward. "You'd be wise to ride on while you can. It will get worse before it gets better."

"Did you know, sir, that some of the Apaches have gotten their hands on the hard stuff?" Benjamin asked.

Kendall came around the dry goods. "You're sure? Damn. I've tried to keep an eye on things, but I can't be everywhere at once."

"Send to Fort Union for a company of soldiers," Fargo suggested. It would take at least that many to keep a lid on things.

"Do you think I don't want troops here?" Kendall responded. "I do, but the organizer of the Great Footrace convinced the governor that it would stir up the Apaches and the Navajos. So the governor put pressure on Colonel Canby, and now I'm on my own. Damn that idiot all to hell."

"He's only trying to avoid bloodshed." Ivy came to her employer's defense.

"So he claims," Niles Kendall said. "But he's going about it in a mighty peculiar way. If you ask me, that journalist wouldn't mind a little bloodletting. It would make for a better story."

To their rear rose a harsh laugh. "Did my ears deceive me, Niles, old friend, or am I the topic of your discussion?"

Fargo turned, and found himself face-to-face with none other than Frank Stockwell.

9

The mastermind behind the Great Footrace was a runt of a man whose features were so much like those of a rodent that Fargo half expected to see long whiskers twitching under Stockwell's thin nose. Beady eyes glittered like burning coals. Pale, high cheekbones glistened as if caked with oil. When Stockwell smiled, small, tapered teeth were revealed. His clothes were typical city attire; shiny shoes, a gray suit that added to his ratlike appearance, and a small-brimmed hat with a crease in the crown, a hat westerners called a muley.

"Frank Stockwell," the man introduced himself, holding out his hand for Fargo to shake. "I don't believe I've had the pleasure of making your acquaintance, sir."

Fargo was one of those who believed that a person's handshake was a key to their character. So he was not surprised to find Stockwell had a cold, clammy palm. Before he could introduce himself, Ivy did it for him.

"This is Skye Fargo, the Trailsman."

Stockwell's eyes glittered more brightly. "Is that a fact?" he said, pumping Fargo's arm with vigor. "Why, everyone has heard of you, sir. It's said that you are a frontiersman of unquestioned courage and integrity. You are a credit to the human race, and I for one am deeply honored to meet you."

Fargo had to hand it to Stockwell. The man was as slick as quicksand and as quick-witted as a fox. "I've heard a lot about you, too," he mentioned.

"None of it flattering, I trust?" Stockwell said, and laughed so loudly and earnestly that several eavesdroppers laughed along with him.

Ivy stepped forward, taking her saddlebags from her shoulder. "Here's the prize money, Mr. Stockwell. I got it here safely, just as I promised I would."

"How many times must I ask you, sweet woman? Call me Frank." Stockwell accepted them, then patted her cheek. "I never doubted you for a minute, Ivy. I know an honest soul when I meet one." He paused. "Did you run into any trouble along the way?"

This time it was Fargo who answered for her. "She nearly got herself killed on account of your stunt, mister. Every curly wolf in the territory was after that money."

Stockwell acted shocked. "Had I known, I can assure you that I never would have proposed the idea." He squeezed her hand. "Thank goodness you did not come to harm. I would be devastated if so lovely a creature were to suffer because of my stupidity."

Fargo almost laughed out loud. Yet Ivy melted, beaming and blushing like a young girl not accustomed to compliments. "The money is safe," she repeated softly.

"More safe than you realize," Stockwell said. Stepping to the counter, he set the saddlebags down. "Tell me, beautiful one. Did you open them?"

"Of course not," Ivy said. "You asked me not to, remember? I gave you my word I wouldn't."

Stockwell unfastened one. "And you always keep your word, I know. A marvelous trait, my dear." His hand slipped into the pouch. "I can only hope that you are as forgiving as you are trustworthy after you learn the truth. You see, I'm afraid that I played a little trick on you and everyone else." Withdrawing his hand, he held the contents for all to see.

Ivy recoiled as if slapped. "That's a pillowcase stuffed with towels!"

"Exactly," Stockwell said. "I wasn't about to risk the prize money. This whole time it has been stored in a safe in my tent."

"But why—" Ivy began, dazed.

"Why the subterfuge?" Stockwell said. "Think, sweet one. The account of your thrilling ride will stir my readers. By embellishing the facts a little, I can make you famous." He gestured, as if writing headlines in the air. "A beautiful damsel alone in the wilds! Fiends lusting for her blood! She must fight for life and limb every foot of the way, and save herself from a fate worse than death!"

Stockwell swelled with excitement and ended his narration with a flourish. If he noticed that no one else shared his enthusiasm, he did not show it.

Ivy's smile withered. "I might have been killed, Frank. And it would have been for nothing!"

"Not at all, sweet one," Stockwell said, draping an arm across her shoulders. "You were on a grand adventure, an escapade meant to inspire and enthrall. Imagine! Every young girl who reads my account will look up to you as the heroine you truly are. Your bravery and resourcefulness will be the talk of the country."

Ivy mellowed, but not Benjamin. "It could just as well have been her death that folks jaw about," he said testily. "What you did was just plain dumb. I ought to put some lead into you to teach you a lesson."

Stockwell did not miss a beat. "Perhaps you should, sir. Perhaps I do deserve to be shot for putting this adorable woman in peril." Taking a step to one side, he held his arms out. "Go ahead! Draw your revolver! Let justice be served! I won't resist!"

Benjamin gaped, as dumbfounded as most everyone else. Ivy, fearing that the muleskinner might just shoot, planted herself in front of Stockwell. "Don't you dare harm a hair on his head! He only did what he thought was right."

Fargo needed fresh air. He strode from the trading post. As he passed through the doorway, he nearly collided with someone who was entering. They stopped abruptly, chest to chest, and he inhaled a fresh minty scent.

It was a young Indian woman, her dress soft buckskin. Raven hair fell past slender shoulders to the small of her curved back. Her body was exquisitely shaped, her upthrust breasts jutting against the buckskin as if striving to burst their bounds. Limpid pools of mystery and allure scrutinized Fargo boldly. "Greetings, white-eye," she said in clipped English. "I not meet you before. How are you known?"

Fargo gave his name, adding, "How about you?"

"Shis-Inday," she said proudly. An Apache, as he had guessed. "I am called Ish-kay-nay."

"The boy?" Fargo ran his eyes over her lush figure again. Whoever had picked her name must have been drunk at the time on *twilt-kay-yee,* an intoxicating drink the Apaches brewed themselves.

She nodded. "When I was little, I hunt with boys, ride with boys, run with boys. I learn all they learn. Now I am strong like the men and fast like the men. I go with them wherever they go."

Ish-kay-nay made the statement with pride, as well she should. Apache men rarely let their women go on raids. To be included, a woman had to be exceptional. And Ish-kay-nay clearly was. She had an air about her, a vitality, that reminded Fargo of thoroughbred horses he had seen in New Orleans.

"You have come to watch the race?" he asked.

Her chin lifted. "I will run *in* it, white-eye, and I will win." She cocked her head. "You are most pleasing to look at. For a white man, you are most handsome. Have you a woman of your own?"

Amused by her brazenness, Fargo said, "No. And I'm not in the market for one, either."

"We have much in common, then," Ish-kay-nay said, and brushed past him, her rich hair swirling. "Maybe we will meet again."

Fargo ambled to the corner and leaned against the wall. Now that Ivy was no longer in peril, what should he do next? It was plain to him, if not to her, that Frank Stockwell was up to no good. Stockwell was a suave confidence man, a swindler whose devious scheming might spark widespread bloodshed unless someone kept an eye on him. Since there was no one else to do the job, Fargo appointed himself.

Out of the trading post came the sidewinder in question, along with Niles Kendall, Ivy, and Benjamin. Kendall caught sight of Fargo and motioned.

"We could use some help. I have an idea who is to blame for selling coffin varnish to the Indians, and where we can find him."

"Count me in," Fargo said. It was an excuse to stay close to Stockwell and maybe glean clues as to what the scalawag was plotting.

Kendall made straight for the gate, then around the palisade and into the woods to the east. A band of Maricopas watched them go by with interest. Beyond the Maricopa camp was a hill, and filing from a ravine at the bottom, cradling whiskey bottles, were half a dozen Apaches, Navajos, and others. At the sight of Kendall, most of the warriors tried to hide what they were carrying. It was no use. Kendall snatched the whiskey and dashed each and every bottle on the ground. Some of the warriors were upset, but none lifted a finger against him.

"They know how I feel about rotgut!" the trader fumed. "Everyone does! Normally, no one would think of bucking me. But now, with all the confusion, someone thinks he can pull the wool over my eyes. He's in for a surprise."

Into the ravine Kendall hastened, stomping like an angry bull. Fargo was only a few steps behind him when Kendall pushed past several Pimas and around a bend.

Ahead, the ravine widened. Parked in the middle of the open space was a flatbed wagon, the bed filled to the brim with crates that bore the words FARMING IMPLEMENTS. One of the crates was open, and from it a stocky man with a scruffy beard was raising a full whiskey bottle. Around the wagon were twenty or thirty warriors waiting their turn to buy firewater.

"Scadding!" Kendall roared.

The man on the wagon glanced up and scowled. Two whites at the back of the wagon moved to the side, rifles held in the crooks of their elbows.

"I warned you the last time I caught you!" the trader declared, halting. "No one is to sell whiskey to the Indians. Ever."

Scadding hefted the bottle. His other hand slipped to his belt, inches from a Remington. "A man has to make a living. And this is how I make mine."

"Get down from there," Kendall said. "I intend to confiscate your wagon and turn you over to Colonel Canby. You've endangered us all."

The whiskey runner was not intimidated. "Hold on, hoss. You might have the right to keep me from selling whiskey at the trading post, but not out here. I'm half a mile away. You don't own this land. I'm free to do as I damn well choose."

Kendall put a hand on his revolver. "You're breaking the law, no matter where you do it."

Fargo took a few steps to the left. Ivy and Benjamin had come around the bend and were moving to the right. Frank Stockwell was the last to appear, and when he did, Scadding grinned, then instantly erased it. What was that all about? Fargo mused.

"So what if I am?" the whiskey runner growled at the trader. "You're not the law. You don't wear a badge. You have no cause to butt into my business."

"I'm a citizen. I have every right to stop a lawbreaker whenever and wherever it is necessary," Kendall said. "Now step down and turn over your hardware."

Another white man waded through the warriors, who were prudently backing off. The newcomer was burly and scarred and held a shotgun. "What's going on, Lucius? This fat man aggravating you?"

"He sure is," Scadding said. "He seems to think he's the Almighty and can push folks around as he pleases. Show him that he can't, Fenner."

Fenner started to level the shotgun. "You heard him, fat man. Take your friends and get the hell out of here before I blow your legs off at the knees."

Niles Kendall and the others froze, but not Fargo. He knew they must not let the burly hardcase get the drop on them. So as the shotgun lowered, his right hand streaked up and out. His thumb jerked the hammer as the Colt cleared leather, his finger tightening the next split second.

At the blast, Fenner twisted as if punched. Scadding dropped the whiskey bottle while going for his revolver. The other underlings ducked for cover beside the wagon, working their rifles.

The ravine rocked to gunfire. Ivy drew and put two shots into Scadding before he got off one of his own. Benjamin fired at the men by the wagon. Kendall staggered, hit in the side. Frank Stockwell, with remarkable agility, dodged around the bend.

Fargo was in motion, sidestepping, firing. Lead buzzed his ear as he banged a shot at a rifleman, who crumpled. Fenner, though, was still very much alive and still a much greater threat, thanks to the shotgun. Livid, Fenner faced Fargo and brought the stock to his shoulder.

The Trailsman fired first. The slug kicked Fenner's head back. His arms flung up, his trigger finger closing in reflex. The shotgun discharged into the air, booming like thunder.

Fargo pivoted toward Scadding and the other rifleman, but they were already down. Scadding dangled from the bed, scarlet drops splattering the soil under him. Gunsmoke wreathed the wagon, tendrils floating toward the clustered warriors. One of the fallen riflemen groaned.

Benjamin and Ivy moved forward, ready to shoot. Kendall had sank to one knee but now he rose, grimacing, a hand pressed to his shirt.

"How bad is it?" Ivy asked.

"Just a crease," the trader said. Passing them, he seized hold of Scadding and dumped him on the ground. "I should have shot you the first time I caught you!" he declared, and hiked a foot as if to stomp on the body. At the last moment he caught himself.

Footsteps behind them brought Fargo around in a twinkling. It was only Frank Stockwell, as composed and calculating as ever.

"Is the horrible affair over, my good friends?"

Niles Kendall was climbing onto the wagon. "Where the hell were you? Why didn't you help?" Puffing, he gained the seat. "There won't be any footrace if the Indians get liquored up and go at each other's throats."

Stockwell unbuttoned his jacket and held the flaps wide. "What would you have me do? As you can see, I am not armed. I'm a journalist, not a gunfighter."

"I'm no gun shark, either," Kendall said, "but I stand up for what I believe." Inspecting a bottle, he suddenly hurled it at nearby boulders and smiled somberly when it smashed to bits. "A pox on Scadding and his kind! They don't give a damn how many lives are lost, just so they earn their blood money."

"Deplorable," Stockwell said. "I share your indignation, sir. And when I write my account of this glorious battle, everyone will learn how honorable you are, and how brave you were to confront these ruffians."

Fargo stared at Scadding. Why had the whiskey runner grinned when Stockwell showed up? Did the two know each other? It did not seem likely.

"We'll burn the wagon," Kendall proposed. "Whiskey and all."

"No!" Stockwell said, a trifle too loudly. "I mean, wouldn't it be wiser to keep the crates as evidence? Won't the authorities need proof that you were justified in doing what you did?"

"This isn't New York City or Chicago," Kendall said. "We're not as fussy about going by the letter of the law." From the crate he plucked some of the paper packing material in which the whiskey bottles had been cushioned, and spread it over the wagon. "Give me a hand."

Stockwell did no such thing, but Ivy and Benjamin climbed up to help. Fargo stood back, reloading the Colt, as the Apaches, Navajos, Pimas, and Maricopas went past. Not one warrior raised a voice in protest. Inscrutable, they hardly gave the dead men a second look.

The rifleman who had been wounded was groaning louder. Fargo dragged him to a boulder and propped him against it. Parting the man's shirt, Fargo examined the wound. There was no hope. The slug had ripped through the stomach, been deflected off a lower rib, and torn into the higher organs. Blood gushed without letup.

"Water. Please. Some water."

Fargo went to the wagon and checked under the seat, then in the box. The only liquid to be had was whiskey. He took a bottle to the boulder, crouched, and opened it. "This is the best I can do."

The man did not reply. He was past feeling thirst, or any other sensation. Eyes blank, mouth agape, he had given up the ghost.

Frank Stockwell was over by the bend, and he did not appear pleased by the outcome. Fingers entwined behind his back, he paced like a cornered panther. The oily smile and counterfeit friendliness were gone.

"This should do us," Niles Kendall said, after the crates were covered. He patted his pockets. "I'm plumb out of matches. Anyone have something we can use?"

"How about these," Benjamin said, taking a flint and steel from the rawhide possibles bag he always wore slung across his chest.

"You do the honors."

The muleskinner hunkered and delivered a few slicing blows to the flint with the oval fire steel. Sparks showered onto the paper. At the first puffs of smoke, Benjamin bent and blew lightly on the material. He was adept at fanning the tiny flames that soon sprouted. Within no time one of the crates was ablaze. He hopped down.

"What a tragic waste of fine whiskey," Frank Stockwell said. In a huff, he wheeled to depart. Ivy stopped him by calling his name.

"What about me, Mr. Stockwell?"

The journalist gruffly responded, "What *about* you, Miss Cambridge? I'm a busy man. Please get to the point."

"Do you have any other work for me? Or do I take it that I'm on my own?" Ivy shuffled her feet. "Plus there's the little matter of the money you owe me."

Stockwell softened in the blink of an eye. Grinning, he said, "How rude of me, my dear. I'm afraid that I'm not accustomed to seeing blood spilled. Please excuse my awful behavior." Walking over, he wrapped an arm around her waist and gave a playful squeeze. "Tell you what. Come with me and we'll discuss your pay and certain other important matters." His voice lowered in mock secrecy. "Just between the two of us, there is another task I have in mind for you. It pays almost as well. Are you interested?"

"Does a bear like honey?"

Fargo did not like how Stockwell's gaze devoured Ivy's figure as they walked off. Couldn't she see that the man was a polecat through and through? That he couldn't be trusted any farther than she could fling a bull buffalo?

Evidently, Benjamin agreed. "Why is it," the muleskinner observed, "that some people can't see the forest for the trees?"

Crackling and hissing filled the ravine as the fire ate the wagon. Kendall had retreated because of the heat and the growing column of smoke. He stood next to the bodies Benjamin had lined up, and said, "Folks believe what they want to believe. You could talk yourself blue in the face, and that young lady wouldn't listen."

Fargo saw no need to linger. He followed the trail to the Bosque Redondo. Now and again he glimpsed Ivy and Stockwell, the newspaper reporter talking and gesturing as if they were the best of friends. They entered the trading post but he strolled past the gate to the huge tent. Out front were the same pair of doves. A brunette whose dress was close to popping at the seams grabbed his arm and breathed into his ear.

"How do you do, handsome? Care for some company? I'm Sally, and I'm as friendly as can be."

"I'll bet you are," Fargo said. Why not enjoy himself? he thought. He deserved it after the ordeal he had gone through escorting Ivy to the post. Pinching the brunette's bottom, he steered her into the smoke-filled interior where Indians and whites rubbed shoulders at games of chance. Everything from stud poker to roulette was being played.

The jingle of coins and chorus of voices made it hard to hear when Sally whispered again.

"Treat me to a drink, big man. I'm bone dry."

"I didn't think whiskey was allowed here."

"It's not." Sally looked both ways, then whispered in his ear, "But what Niles Kendall doesn't know won't hurt him. The man I work for has cases of it hidden out back."

"Is that so," Fargo said. He decided to tell Kendall after he left. At the moment, though, the idea of a drink appealed to him. Rather than buy the house brand, Fargo led the filly to a narrow gap between the roulette wheel and the side of the tent and showed her the bottle he had taken from Lucius Scadding's wagon. "Will this do?"

Sally thirstily bobbed her chin, but said, "You'd better not. Bascomb, the man who runs this place, doesn't like it when customers bring their own stuff. Either you buy from him or he kicks you out."

Fargo opened the bottle and tilted it to his lips. He was sick and tired of others trying to run roughshod over him. As the whiskey burned a path down his throat to warm his stomach, he relaxed for the first time in days. He should have known it would not last long.

Sally's fingernails bit into his skin. "I tried to warn you, handsome," she said under her breath. "Now there will be hell to pay."

Shadows fell across them. Fargo stopped drinking and turned. Confronting him were two gunmen and a tall man in fashionable clothes, a man who could pass for a banker or a cattle baron if not for the bullwhip curled in his brawny right hand.

"Let me guess. You're Bascomb."

The man nodded. "You should have listened to her, jackass," he said, and struck without warning.

10

The only thing that saved Skye Fargo from losing an eye, or worse, was the roulette wheel. That, and the people who were packed into the tent, especially those who hemmed Bascomb in on either side. For in the confined space he could not move freely. His swing was hampered by the press of patrons. The lash, uncurling with lightning speed, clipped the roulette wheel instead of the Trailsman.

Fargo did not give the man a chance to swing again. He hurled the whiskey bottle at Bascomb's face. Predictably, Bascomb dodged. At the same moment the two gunmen hurtled forward to protect their boss. As they did, Fargo threw himself at the roulette wheel. His fingers found a grip along the edge of the table it rested on. With a powerful heave he upended both, flinging the wheel and the table it rested on into the path of the onrushing gunmen.

Women screamed. Men cursed. Those who were nearby pushed and shoved to get elsewhere, starting a panic that spread like wildfire. A panic that was fueled when one of the gunmen, struggling to get out from under the roulette wheel, snapped off a wild shot that missed Fargo and ripped through the tent.

A single stride brought Fargo to the shooter. Cocking a leg, he smashed his boot into the man's jaw and the gunman collapsed.

The second gunman had the full weight of the roulette wheel on his chest and was momentarily helpless.

That left Bascomb, who, with a roar of fury, charged, clubbing Fargo with the bullwhip's handle. Fargo brought up an arm, blocking a rain of blows as he backpedaled to give himself room to move.

"You're worm food, mister! Do you hear me? Worm, food!"

Fargo backed against the tent. Bascomb hiked his arm to strike again, and instantly Fargo ducked and dived, tackling Bascomb around the shins. They crashed to the ground, Bascomb flailing at Fargo's head and shoulders but inflicting little pain. For his part, Fargo tried to grab the man's arm, but it was like trying to seize a slick eel.

Vaguely, Fargo was aware that most of the gamblers were fleeing pell-mell from the big tent. In the process, some fell and were trampled. Chairs were splintered. Tables toppled with resounding crashes. Someone shouted for everyone to stay calm, but the frightened mob did not heed.

Bascomb landed a solid blow at last. Dazed, Fargo heaved, pushing the man from him, then scrambled to his knees. Bascomb also half rose. The lash swept at Fargo's face, and this time there was no roulette wheel to block it.

Fargo dived under the whip. He felt it bite into the flesh between his shoulder blades. Then he landed on his shoulder and rolled. Bracing his soles, he catapulted upward, his shoulder muscles bunched, his right fist clenched so tight his knuckles were white.

Straightening as he unwound, Fargo planted a right cross on the tip of Bascomb's jaw. Backed by his full weight and the steely sinews that corded his frame, the punch lifted Bascomb clean off his feet.

Bascomb flew a good yard, smashing into a table as he came down. One of the legs snapped and the table fell on top of him.

Fargo lurched erect. The gunman who had been pinned was now free and stabbing for the Smith & Wesson on his hip. Fargo's Colt flashed out. At the click of the hammer, the gunman imitated a tree, eyes wide with fear.

"Don't shoot, mister!"

"Unbuckle your gunbelt," Fargo commanded.

The man obeyed and stood, arms elevated. "Don't shoot, please," he repeated. "Bascomb doesn't pay me enough to die for him."

Fargo shifted. The gunman's employer had been stunned and was feebly trying to rise, the bullwhip lying forgotten a few feet away. Fargo kicked him in the chest and Bascomb sprawled backward. "Just stay where you are," he warned.

The general panic was subsiding. Most of the customers were gone. Those who remained lined the tent walls, or were picking themselves up from the dirt floor. A few were unconscious.

For once Fargo was not sure of what to do. He had half a mind to run Bascomb off, and every other gambler and whiskey peddler he could find. But he had no legal right to do so. He wasn't a lawman, or attached to the army any longer. "Kendall is going to hear about the whiskey you've been selling," he said, and backed out, covering Bascomb and the gunman until he was past the flap.

Holstering the Colt, Fargo made for the trading post. Niles Kendall was sitting on a powder keg. The Great Footrace threatened to turn into a Great Bloodbath unless something was done. Troops should be sent for, whether Frank Stockwell liked it or not.

A clerk told Fargo that Kendall was not back yet. The trader had probably stayed at the ravine to make sure that the whiskey wagon burned to the ground. Fargo headed for the Ovaro, intending to ride out there. As he stepped off the porch, Ivy Cambridge appeared out of the throng, smiling and waving a red bandanna. Around her left arm she had tied another. Behind her was Stockwell.

"Skye! There you are! I've been looking for you!" Ivy grasped his hand and pulled him over to the building, where they were out of the way. She seemed excited about something. "How would you like a job?"

"What kind?" Fargo inquired.

Stockwell reached them. He looked none too pleased. "What's this?" he demanded. "When you asked if it would be all right to have a helper, I assumed that you meant your muleskinner friend Benjamin."

"I'll ask him, too," Ivy said. "The more, the better, right?"

Frank Stockwell's jaw muscles twitched. "Of course, my dear. But why bother Mr. Fargo? He must have much more important business to attend to. Let's go find someone else."

"I want Skye," Ivy insisted, and shoved the spare red bandanna into Fargo's hand. "Hear me out. That's all I ask." In a rush, she went on. "Mr. Stockwell has hired me to be a—" She paused and glanced at the journalist. "What did you call it again?"

"A referee, of sorts. Like they have at boxing contests and the like." Stockwell puffed up his chest. "The actual judging will be left to me, of course. I, and I alone, will pick the winner."

"A referee," Ivy reiterated. "I'm to keep the peace during the race. Make sure no one cheats. That sort of thing." She tapped the bandanna tied to her arm. "This is kind of like my badge. Everyone who works with me gets to wear one so folks will know who we are." She gazed deep into Fargo's eyes. "Are you interested, Skye? There's a hundred dollars in it for everyone who hires on."

Fargo fingered the bandanna, pondering. What was Frank Stockwell up to? Having referees made sense, but why Ivy? She could take care of herself ably enough, but she would be hopelessly over her head if the Apaches or the Navajos acted up. Did Stockwell have a hidden motive? If so, there was only one way to learn what it was. "I'll do it," he said, "on one condition."

"What might that be?" Ivy asked.

"We should have the right to do more than just make sure the runners obey the rules," Fargo said, facing Stockwell. "We need to be able to keep the peace at the trading post and the Indian camps. Give us the right to patrol the entire Bosque Redondo."

The journalist laughed. "Really, sir. I'm not the governor, or a general. I don't have the power to invest such authority in you or anyone else."

"This isn't back East. Here, we make our own rules. Since the Great Footrace was your idea, and the governor left you in charge, you can do as you see fit." It tickled Fargo to see Stockwell squirm. "You were at the ravine. Something needs to be done, or the race might never be held."

"Skye has a point," Ivy said.

"We need soldiers," Fargo pressed. "But the next best thing would be a group of regulators who can drive troublemakers off. What do you say?"

Stockwell was on the spot. He scanned the people milling in front of the trading post, and frowned. "I suppose it wouldn't hurt," he conceded. "But no more than three or four of you. And remember, no one gets paid until after the race."

"Why then?" Fargo asked.

Ivy answered. "He already explained that to me. Frank has to keep track of every penny he spends. It will be easier for him to hand out what's due all at once." She sighed. "I don't even get my courier pay until then."

Fargo doubted he would ever see the hundred dollars, but he tied the red bandanna around his left arm above the elbow. "It's settled then. We'll get one of the clerks to write up a poster and nail it to the gate. By nightfall everyone will know."

"An excellent suggestion," Stockwell said, but he did not look nearly as delighted as he tried to sound. Excusing himself, he departed.

Ivy watched him go with longing on her face. "Isn't he just about the finest human being you've ever met?" She tapped the bandanna again. "Imagine. Him having so much faith in me that he trusts me to keep the peace."

"It would be smarter to have troops here," Fargo brought up, and let it go at that. To say anything bad about Stockwell would only anger her. Some lessons had to be learned the hard way, and this was one.

"So what should we do first?" Ivy wanted to know.

Fargo did not waste another moment. The big tent was filling when they got there. Bascomb sat on a chair, dabbing a gash on his forehead with a handkerchief. The gunman Fargo had kicked was still out cold, while the other one was nowhere around.

"You've got your nerve, coming back in here!" Bascomb snapped on seeing Fargo enter. "What the hell do you want?"

"We have the authority to close you down," Fargo informed him. "And that's just what we're doing."

"Like hell!" Bascomb shot out of the chair. "Who gave you this authority? Kendall?"

"The man who organized the race. And he got his from the territorial governor."

"Frank Stockwell?" Bascomb said, and snorted. "What is this, mister? Some kind of joke? Does he want a bigger cut? Why didn't he just say so?"

"Cut?" Ivy said.

"Don't play innocent with me, lady," Bascomb said. "If you're working for Stockwell, then you must know he's the one who brought me here. In return for fifty percent of the take, naturally."

Ivy turned pale. "You're lying."

"Like hell I am. Just ask Stockwell. He showed up in my saloon in Taos about a month ago. Went on and on about how much *dinero* the two of us could make if we partnered up. All I had to do was set up a few gaming tables and milk the pilgrims for every *centavo* I could wring out of them." Bascomb surveyed the wreckage. "He promised me protection, lady. He said that so long as I didn't kill anyone, I could pretty much do as I pleased."

Fargo remembered the look that Lucius Scadding had given Stockwell. "You're not the only one he talked into coming, are you?"

"Are you kidding? That jasper doesn't miss a trick. He's brought in half the gamblers in the territory, along with enough whiskey peddlers to keep the stinking redskins drunk for a year." Chuckling, Bascomb said, "I have to hand it to him. For a dude, he's mighty shrewd. He'll make a fortune, counting the prize money."

Ivy took a step nearer. "What about it?"

Bascomb glanced from her to Fargo and back again. "Wait a minute. What is this? If you're really working for Stockwell, you should know this stuff already."

"I want you to come with us," Ivy said. "I want you to repeat what you just said in front of Frank Stockwell."

"Why should I?" Bascomb said, continuing to slowly back away. "Something ain't right here. I don't know what it is, but I want no part of it." His right hand dipped under his jacket. "Get out, both of you. Tell Stockwell that he has to come here in person. I don't care if he doesn't want to be seen in public with me."

More and more pieces of the puzzle were fitting together. Enough to prove to Fargo that Stockwell's scheme was far grander than he had suspected. The man had every angle covered, from the gambling to the booze. And who knew what else?

"Please," Ivy insisted, taking another step. "All I want is to give Mr. Stockwell the chance to show that you're lying. He's too honorable to ever stoop so low."

"Honorable? Frank Stockwell?" Bascomb snorted, his hand now fully out of sight. "Lady, you're *loco*. Stockwell would murder his own mother if there was money in it. He's pulled the wool over everyone's eyes, from the governor on down. If you were really working for him, you wouldn't be so stupid."

"I am working for him," Ivy declared.

"Bull," Bascomb said, and drew. A short-barreled pistol gleamed with nickel plating. He had it out and cocked before she could bat an eye.

As fast as the gambler was, Skye Fargo was faster. His Colt thundered, the impact jolting Bascomb backward. The nickel-plated pistol went off, seemingly wide of the mark, and Fargo fired again, adding a new nostril to the gambler's features. Bascomb wilted, the fancy revolver sprinkled with red freckles.

Fargo rotated on the balls of his feet. No one else was inclined to interfere. "How do you feel about Stockwell now?" he asked Ivy, and when she did not answer he swung around.

Cambridge was on the ground, a hand over a wound in her left thigh. Torment marred her lovely features. Gaping at the gambler, she said, aghast, "It can't be. It can't be. It just can't."

Kneeling, Fargo moved her hand to probe the gunshot. The bullet had gone through the fleshy outer part of her leg. Little blood was evident. "It's not serious," he said. "But let's get you to the trading post. Kendall will have what we need to tend it."

"No," Ivy said, clutching at his shirt when he began to rise. "Take me out of here."

"Where to?"

"Anywhere." Her fingers dug into him. "I need a little time to myself. Time to think. Time to sort everything out." She pulled him lower, desperation tinging her tone. "Please, Skye. *Please*."

"What about Benjamin?"

She misunderstood. "I want *you* to take me. And if you won't, then I'll go by myself." Grunting, she propped an arm under her hip and shoved upright. Unable to bear her full weight on the hurt leg, she tottered and would have fallen had he not thrown an arm around her midsection.

"I've got you," Fargo said. Ivy sagged against him, suddenly as weak as a kitten, her eyes closing. He guided her from the tent and into the trading post. A lot of stares were cast at them but they were left alone. They reached their horses without incident. Helping her onto the dun, he forked leather. Once past the gate, he rode south, keeping an eye on Ivy, who had to grip the saddle horn to stay on her mount.

Navajos were camped south of Sumner's. Warriors, women, and children stopped whatever they were doing to study Fargo and the blonde. Once friendly to whites, the tribe had grown more and more hostile as the years went by.

Fargo did not blame them. They were tired of having their best land taken by settlers, tired of being denied the right to hunt in areas they formerly roamed at will, and upset because there was a lot of talk about forcing them onto a reservation. Sooner or later, they would stop bending over backward to please the whites. When that happened, when their patience snapped, widespread bloodshed would be the result.

Beyond the camp, Fargo slowed to confirm that none of the warriors were shadowing them. Urging the pinto into a trot, he forged on until Ivy commenced to sway and nod off now and again. By then they were twelve miles from the trading post. The trees had thinned but ample cover existed. In a glade ringed by thickets, he drew rein. "This is as far as we go," he announced.

The sun was poised on the western rim of the world. Fargo gently lowered Ivy, spread out her bedroll, and made her sit. She mumbled her thanks, her eyelids hooded, exhausted—or ill. Fargo felt her forehead, which burned to the touch. "I need to examine your wound," he said.

"I'm fine," Ivy replied. "It hardly hurts anymore."

Fargo was not taking no for an answer. Sliding the toothpick from under his boot, he applied the tip to the fabric and carefully slit it wide enough to inspect the bullet hole. As he had feared, it was inflamed and swollen. "Infection is setting in. Strip out of your pants while I boil water."

"My pants?" Ivy said and giggled giddily. "This isn't a trick to get me under the blankets, is it?"

"Cover yourself when you're done. I'll be right back." Fargo hurried to the Pecos. Dipping his coffeepot into the sluggish current, he filled it and returned.

It had been a mistake to leave Sumner's, Fargo scolded himself. Ivy was in dire need, and Kendall was bound to know someone with doctoring skills.

Few greenhorns were aware that infection from gunshots killed more people than bullets did, only more slowly, and much more painfully. Fargo had recently seen a man die from just such a wound. The afflicted arm had swollen to three times its normal size, and the man had been in so much agony that it had taken three men to hold him down so medicine could be administered. Unfortunately, gangrene set in, and the man had died after three days of constant anguish, wailing pitiably for hours at the end.

Fargo would spare Ivy that if he could. She had slid off her pants and left them beside her blanket. Hunkering, he lifted it just high enough to expose the wound. Swelling had started. By morning, if all did not go well, pus would be oozing out, and the skin would discolor.

"I don't feel good," Ivy mumbled, then smacked her lips.

Her forehead was hotter. Fargo soaked his own bandanna with cold water, folded it, and applied it to her brow. While the coffeepot heated up, he tried to entice her into eating some jerky but she clamped her mouth shut.

Fargo left to search under the trees for a stick the right length and width. To save her life, he must inflict agony unlike any she had ever suffered. In due course he found the one he wanted.

Ivy had fallen asleep. Fargo slid a rock close to the fire, trimmed the stick to a sharp point, and propped it on the rock so that the flames charred the tip. When the water was boiling, he woke her. She was drowsy and sluggish and swatted at his hands when he sat her up.

"Go away, Skye. I'm too tired right now."

"I'm sorry," Fargo said. "This has to be done." He washed the wound, then wadded the hem of the blanket and held it toward her. "You might want to bite down on this."

"What are you fixing to do?" Ivy asked, her drowsiness evaporating like dew under the blazing sun when she saw him pick up the smoking stick. "No!"

"It's the surest way I know." Gingerly lowering a knee onto her leg below her thigh, he held the tip close to the hole.

Ivy plucked at his sleeve. "This isn't necessary! Really. By morning I'll be as good as new."

"Bite down," Fargo insisted, and when she did, he promptly plunged the stick into the wound. Loud hissing ensued. The stench of burning flesh assailed him. Ivy arched her spine and vented a muffled scream, tears gushing. She grasped his arms, seeking to tear the stick away.

"Stop! No more!" she pleaded.

Fargo withdrew the stick and Ivy sagged, sobbing quietly. She did not see him poke the tip into the flames again, nor notice when he shifted her leg so the exit wound was exposed. Like the entry hole, it showed signs of initial infection. So Fargo gave it the same treatment.

Ivy stiffened and cried out, a strangled shriek that sent roosting birds in nearby trees into raucous flight. She grabbed his wrist but Fargo would not relent. The sizzling gradually faded. Extracting the stick, he cast it into the darkness.

Suddenly Ivy fainted. Catching hold, Fargo lowered her onto her saddle. After hiking the blanket up around her chin, he made himself some coffee.

It was close to midnight when Ivy groaned and came around. Blinking at him, she said thickly, "I's sorry for being such a fool."

"Don't be so hard on yourself. I've known grown men who couldn't hold up to the pain as well as you did."

"Not that," Ivy said. Biting her lower lip, she gazed skyward. "I sure can pick them, can't I? First Tom Grifter, now Frank Stockwell. I must have a secret hankering to spend my whole life miserable."

What could Fargo say? He sat staring out over the Pecos, listening to the water gurgle and lap against a rocky point. It was a minute or two before he realized new sounds were mixed with those of the river. Low, choking sobs, grew steadily louder. Ivy had buried her face in her hands and was releasing grief she had pent up for years. She cried and cried and cried, pausing only once to ask a question for which Fargo had no answer.

"Why the hell is life so damn unfair?"

11

Chirping birds woke the Trailsman when pink streaks tinged the eastern sky. Raising, he rekindled the fire and put coffee on. Ivy Cambridge was sleeping peacefully, and he did not disturb her. She needed all the rest she could get.

Ivy's fever had broken in the middle of the night. Fargo had examined her every hour or so, and applied the moistened bandanna many times. With the fever and swelling gone, she would recover rapidly. For a few days she would be stiff and sore, but by the end of the month she would be as fit as ever.

Presently, the sun rose. Ivy slept on. Fargo checked on the horses, made a circuit of the glade, and ate a breakfast of scalding black coffee and jerky. It was past nine, by his reckoning, and the temperature was starting to climb, when the sight of the Pecos sparked an idea.

Fargo had a habit that struck some of his frontiersmen friends as comical. He liked to take regular baths. In a day and age when many mountain men and trappers would routinely go a whole year without bathing, his habit was considered downright peculiar.

Cleanliness was not next to godliness on the frontier. A hot bath was a luxury in which few indulged. It was commonly believed, by mountain men and settlers alike, that too much bathing was bad for the health. It made a person sickly. So to get a mountain man to bathe took a lot of persuasion, or a lot of liquor.

Fargo bucked the trend. He did not like being grungy, or going through life smelling like the Ovaro. Whenever he could, he indulged in a bath. And here was a golden opportunity.

At a secluded nook along the shore, he stripped off his boots and buckskins, laid the Henry and the Colt on top of the pile at the water's edge, and waded in. His body broke out in goose bumps. The water was quite cold compared to the air. He went further, until the river rose as high as his waist. Then, taking a breath, he submerged and squatted there half a minute, the water tingling his skin.

Breaking the surface, Fargo swam upriver a short distance, and back again. He took his sweet time, enjoying the rare tranquility. As he drew abreast of the nook where his clothes lay, a shadowy figure detached itself from the trees. Fargo veered landward, stroking cleanly, making for his guns.

The figure limped into the sunlight. Ivy Cambridge, rumpled and tired but undeniably gorgeous, smiled sheepishly. "I saw you swimming and thought I would join you."

Stopping a ways out, Fargo responded, "Are you delirious? What you need is more rest. It won't take much to start that leg bleeding again. Go back and crawl under your blankets."

Ivy hobbled to the river's edge. "I'm not about to jump in and act the fool," she said. "But I feel dirty. All that sweating I did, and the dry blood. I need to wash it off."

"I'll leave so you can do it in private," Fargo offered, and moved toward the bank.

Ivy gaped as if dumbstruck as his shoulders and chest emerged. Her eyes lingered on the corded muscles of his arms and torso, and she swallowed hard when the upper half of his finely muscled abdomen rose into view. "Lordy, you're beautiful!" she breathed.

Fargo hesitated. Any other woman, and he would have had no qualms about marching right out, buck naked. But Ivy was different. She had been through so much in her life, had suffered so greatly. "Maybe you should turn your back while I get dressed."

To his amazement, Ivy fumbled at her shirt, undoing the buttons.

"What do you think you're doing?"

Ivy did not answer. Bowing her chin, she removed the shirt and started on the rest of her clothes. She did not look up until she was bare to the world. Her cheeks were beet red and she was breathing heavily.

Despite himself, Fargo was mesmerized. Her body was exquisite. Perfect breasts thrust hardening nipples outward. A flat stomach crowned a golden bush at the junction of slender, glorious thighs. The bullet hole stood out against the backdrop of creamy flesh, and she covered it with a hand as she slowly shuffled into the Pecos.

Fargo did not move. He was torn between desire and concern. And, too, his manhood had stirred. If the water dropped any lower, his lust would be obvious. Giving her one more chance to change her mind, he said, "Think about this. It's hardly the right time or place."

Ivy waded closer, her breasts rising and falling with each deep breath. It was hard to tell whether she was scared or cold or both. Her blush deepened, and when she was at arm's length from him, she halted. "So beautiful," she repeated.

Fargo could not reply if he wanted to. His throat felt uncommonly dry and had a lump in it the size of an apple. He actually gave a start when Ivy reached out and gingerly brushed her fingertips across his chest.

"So smooth," Ivy said softly. "You're not all hairy, like Tom was." She pressed her palm flat and swirled it in tiny circles, dipping lower and lower until it was on his muscled abdomen. "You're so hard, too."

If she only knew! Fargo shifted, eager to crush her to him. But he dared not, not with her leg in the condition it was in.

She stepped closer. Now her nipples were almost touching him, and her warm breath fanned his neck and chin. "I've wanted to do this since the moment we met," she said in a whisper. "But I was afraid. Afraid that you would be just like Tom. That you would beat me and—"

Fargo placed a finger on her lips. "Hush. All that is behind you now. You can't let the past spoil your future."

Ivy kissed his finger. Then, to his surprise, she grasped it and inserted it into her mouth. Sliding it up and down, she glided her tongue over its entire length. Hungrily, her gaze roved lower, lingering on what the water hid.

Rock steady, in more ways than one, Fargo lightly placed his left hand on her right breast and tweaked the nipple. Ivy squirmed. Withdrawing his finger, she sighed and closed her eyes. "I've dreamed of this moment," she said huskily.

Fargo cupped her other breast. He was not paying attention to her hands, so he was considerably startled when warm fingers wrapped around his pole and others cupped him, lower down. He had not expected her to be so bold.

"So big," Ivy cooed. Her hand languidly stroked him, triggering a sensation Fargo had to fight to control. It was too soon. Gritting his teeth, he held the premature explosion back. After a bit the sensation passed and he could breathe normally again.

Ivy was staring at him in mixed awe, and something else. "I don't really hate men, you know," she confided. "It's just that—"

This time Fargo silenced her with a kiss. Her lips molded to his and she greedily sucked his tongue into her mouth.

Her velvet tongue entwined with his, swirling it, tasting it. A long, low moan escaped her as his right hand massaged her breasts and his left roamed to her buttocks and cupped them. He pressed against her, the heat of her body incredible. She let go of his organ. Her hands rose to his shoulders and she clung to him as a drowning person might cling to a log.

Their kiss lasted forever. When they parted, Ivy was panting and quivering, her eyes hooded with raw passion. "It's never been like this before. My head is all jumbled inside."

Fargo kissed her cheek, her throat, her ear. He nibbled the lobe, feeling her wriggle. Her fingers gripped his hair and twisted so hard that it hurt. She was flush against him, soft and smooth and inviting, her fear eclipsed by unbridled carnal cravings.

Fargo had to remind himself to be gentle. He suppressed an urge to carry her to the bank and take her there on the grass, roughly, wildly. Her leg would not bear the strain. Instead, he explored every square inch of her pulsing form. He lathered her nipples and squeezed her inner thighs. He rubbed her belly, her bush. When at long, long last he slid a finger between her legs and lightly brushed her nether lips, she stiffened and gasped, tears filling her eyes.

"Ohhhhhhh! It's been so long!"

Touching her core shattered what little was left of the inner dam that had held her sensual hunger in check for so long. She kissed and bit and sucked and licked, unable to get enough of him. Her hands were everywhere, front, back, and below. She aroused a feverish inferno in him, and he repaid the favor.

"More! More!"

Fargo slid his hand to Ivy's slit. Her breasts mashed against him when he gingerly inserted a finger. Her teeth clamped on his shoulder, breaking the skin. At the first stroke, she heaved upward, forgetting about her wounded leg. It buckled slightly, and she cried out.

To keep her from hurting herself, Fargo gripped Ivy by the hips. Holding her steady, he lifted her, counting on the buoyancy of the water to lessen the strain on her limb.

Ivy had a better idea. Widening her legs, she hunched her bottom down and in. The angle was just right; she impaled herself to the hilt on his throbbing pole. Eyes widening, she tossed back her head and moaned. Her left leg looped around his hip and locked fast.

Fargo could let go to cup both heaving breasts. She was leaning back, lost in ecstasy, her cherry lips in full bloom. The moan became a low-pitched whine.

"So good! So good!"

Bracing himself, Fargo thrust upward. The stroke raised her a good two inches out of the water. Crying out, she met the thrust with a downward plunge. From then on, she could not get enough. She matched his ardor, her body perfectly in tune with his, moving her hips in counterpoint to the driving tempo he established.

Fargo lost track of time. The river, the bank, the trees were all a blur. Supreme pleasure coursed through him, to the exclusion of all else. He stroked and stroked, inwardly building toward an eruption that would pale a volcano's. The slap of their stomachs and the splash of the water were all he heard.

"I'm coming!" Ivy suddenly said, and did so, violently. Her nails raked him, her mouth tried to cover his, but she could not hold still. Pumping and thrashing, she went over the brink.

Following suit, Fargo was lost in a haze of spinning senses and hammering delight. The explosion went on and on. When it finally abated, his temples were drumming and his legs were weak.

Ivy was as limp as a rag. "Thank you," she breathed. "I

never knew it could be like that." Sliding off, she tried to stand but her right leg would not cooperate.

Fargo held her close and waded to shore. Depositing her gently, he reclined on his side and rested until they were dry. She propped her head on his chest and played with his hair, wearing a wide smile. "What's so funny?" he asked.

"I don't reckon I hate men anymore."

Chuckling, Fargo pecked her cheek. As much as he would like to while away the day with her, there was a lot to do before the race. Sitting up, he pulled on his pants. "We have to get back."

"I know." Ivy sighed. Propped on her elbow, she traced a finger along his shoulder. "I'll never forget this day, Trailsman. I'll never forget what you've done for me."

"All I did was be your friend."

"Oh, you did a lot more than that," Ivy disagreed. Rising, she kissed him on the lips, a tender, heartfelt kiss that she was clearly reluctant to break. When she did, she squeezed him and said throatily, "Men like you are few and far between. The gal who finally snares you will be the happiest woman alive, I reckon."

There it was again. No matter what women might say to the contrary, in the back of their minds always lurked the specter of wedlock. But Fargo had made it plain how he felt. He had nothing to be guilty about.

Fully dressed, Fargo adjusted his hat. "You need to eat to keep your strength up. I'll see what I can rustle up."

"No rush," Ivy said, stretching like a contented cat. "I'll be along shortly."

The Ovaro and the dun had their heads up and their ears pricked when Fargo strode into the clearing. He assumed that he was the reason until he realized that they were peering into the woods in a different direction. Instinct warned him a second before a moving shape appeared, and he spun, the Colt springing from its holster as if alive.

"We meet again, white-eye."

Ish-kay-nay was dressed in a shorter buckskin dress than before. Her hair had been tied back, and her face was sleek with sweat. She saw the revolver and smirked.

"Afraid I try to scalp you?"

Fargo replaced the pistol and smiled. "A man can't be too careful these days." He indicated the coffeepot. "My camp is yours. Are you thirsty?"

"Very," Ish-kay-nay admitted, advancing. "But I can not drink until I am done." She mopped her forehead with her sleeve. "Every day I run from when the sun comes up until it is overhead. I practice for the race."

"Alone and unarmed?" Fargo said.

Ish-kay-nay's chin elevated. "I am Shis-Inday," she reminded him. "I fear no man, no animal." Her features clouded. "Men who touch me, I claw their eyes out." To demonstrate, she swiped at the air with her long nails.

Fargo believed her. Apache women were as strong-willed and independent as Apache warriors, and just as fierce when aroused. "I'd never think of touching a woman against her will," he mentioned.

"Not you I mean. I scratched the white-eye who came from beyond the big river. The puny man who wears the scent of flowers, like a woman."

"Frank Stockwell?"

Glowering, Ish-kay-nay nodded. "He sent a man to me last night. Say come talk, very important. So I go to his lodge. But he wanted to sit close to me and have me drink firewater." She darkened at the memory. "He told me I am prettiest woman he ever see. That he is important man, that he give me many fine things. Then he put his hands on me."

Stockwell had been playing with fire. Apache women were famous for their fidelity to their own kind. "Apaches never bed anybody but Apaches," was how an old trapper had once phrased it.

Lightning flared in Ish-kay-nay's eyes. "I teach him. I scratch him, like this," and she imitated what she had done, to demonstrate. A grin spread across her face. "He howled like wolf. Begged me not to kill him."

"Too bad you didn't," Fargo said.

The Mescalero came over. "I like you, white-eye. Maybe after I win money, we spend time together, eh? Just you and me, alone. I know a special place."

"I could be tempted," Fargo said with a straight face. "But it sounds to me like you're counting your chickens before they're hatched. Hundreds have signed up for the footrace. What makes you think you'll be the winner?"

No one could ever accuse Ish-kay-nay of being modest. "I am the best. I am the fastest."

"What would you do with so much money?" Fargo asked. It was more than most whites earned in five years, more than most Apaches saw in a lifetime.

Ish-kay-nay tossed her raven mane. "I care nothing for the colored paper. Winning is all I want. I will think what to do with money after it is mine." She glanced toward the Pecos and grinned. "I leave now. Here comes the one you swam with."

Fargo turned. Ivy was limping toward them, dressed except for her boots, which she held in her left hand. In her right hand was her gunbelt. As the Mescalero's words sank in, it hit him that Ish-kay-nay had seen them together in the river. "You were watching us the whole time?" he asked, but did not receive an answer.

The Apache maiden was no longer there. She sped northward, sprinting flat out. Making it all look so easy, she weaved among the trees as if she were endowed with wings on her feet. Her body was poetry in motion, as graceful as an antelope in flight, as alluring as a Denver showgirl's. She looked back only once to smile and bob a hand.

Fargo returned the gesture.

"I thought that I heard voices," Ivy declared, joining him. "What on earth was she doing here? I've seen her around the trading post from time to time, but I never caught her name."

"She's going to win the race," Fargo said.

"Just like that? Doesn't she know that the fastest runners in the Navajo nation and among her own people are taking part? I've seen some of them practice. She has her work cut out for her."

"So do we. Are you ready to go back?"

"Whenever you are."

They ate first, a rattlesnake that Fargo stumbled on while hunting for deer. He chopped off the head, skinned the body, and cut the meat into bits to use in a stew. Ivy watched it boil, her nose scrunched in distaste.

"I've never had snake before. What does it taste like?"

"Snake."

She was unsure until she had her first taste. A couple of bites was enough to convince her that rattler was as tasty as venison or a buffalo steak. Downing her portion with relish, she asked for a second helping.

Fargo had little fear of Ivy suffering a relapse. With an appetite like that, she would be fully recovered in no time. On the ride north, she chattered constantly, telling him about her childhood and her travels after she fled her father's cane. In a way, he missed the old Ivy, the one who could go a whole day and not say three words.

Little had changed at Sumner's Trading Post. The Apaches, Navajos, Pimas, and Maricopas were still in their respective camps. Activity at the post was as hectic as ever. But the big tent that belonged to Bascomb was gone.

Niles Kendall sat in a rocking chair on the porch, whittling. He had opened his shirt halfway against the heat, revealing that his side had been bandaged. "So there you are!" he declared when they reined up at a hitching rail. "I was afraid you'd lit a shuck without saying *adios.*"

Fargo was wearing the red bandanna on his arm. Explaining what it meant, he asked, "Didn't Stockwell tell you that he hired us to keep the peace?"

"Not a word." Kendall stopped carving. "But I haven't seen much of him since we tangled with Scadding. Last night a bunch of riders showed up late, and I understand he's spent most of the day with them."

Ivy was dismounting when a wiry bundle of buckskin hurtled out the door and wrapped its arms around her. "Missy! Where in tarnation have you been? I heard about the shootin', and I was worried sick."

"I'm fine, Benjamin," Ivy assured the muleskinner. "Never better, in fact." She giggled merrily, which caused Benjamin to step back in confusion.

Fargo squatted next to the rocking chair. "Tell me more about the riders who showed up. Have you seen them?"

"Just one," Kendall said. "A harmless fellow who has a weakness for candy. He came by this morning shortly after I opened up. Inquisitive type, too. Wanted to know if I'd run into Ivy, and if you were anywhere around."

"He have a name?"

"Not that he would reveal. I was tempted to follow him and learn where he was camped, but Stockwell came in and wanted the flags I had ordered for the race." Gazing toward the gate, Kendall said, "Well, speak of the devil."

Attired in a brown suit and wearing a different bowler, Frank Stockwell approached. He twirled a cane while whistling loudly, acting as if he did not have a care in the world. "So here you are," he declared. "I was about ready to find someone else to be my roving referees." Abruptly stopping, he blinked rapidly. The reason was a certain raven-haired beauty talking to a pair of husky Apache warriors over by the south wall.

Ivy had swiveled at the sound of his voice. Her hand on the Smith & Wesson, she was on the verge of drawing when Fargo caught her eye and shook his head. Frowning, Ivy jerked her hand from the gun butt and turned away before the journalist could notice.

"So," Stockwell said to no one in particular, "are we all set for tomorrow?"

Kendall resumed whittling. "The men who are going to be posted along the river will leave at five in the morning. That will give them plenty of time to get into position. Each one will post a flag, just like you asked." He surveyed his establishment. "What with everyone else going to the finish line to be there at the end, my place will be practically deserted. I never do much business the day of the race, but this will be the worst yet."

"Think of all the money you've made already, thanks to my stroke of brilliance," Stockwell said. "All snug and tidy in your safe."

"That's where I keep every penny I've ever earned," Kendall said. "I don't trust banks worth a hoot."

Fargo pretended to have no interest in their conversation, but he did not miss a single word. He was staring out the open gate and saw a scrawny man in a floppy hat mosey into the compound. Spotting Ivy, the man drew up short, gawking, then backed on out of there as if his britches were on fire. As well he should.

It was Zeke.

12

Skye Fargo was down the steps in a bound. He brushed past Frank Stockwell and raced across the compound. Or tried to. The trading post was so thronged with people that he could not take two steps without bumping into someone. Shouldering aside those who got in his way, heedless of the hard stares and oaths that were flung at him, he gained the gate, only to find that Zeke was nowhere to be seen.

"Damn," Fargo said and jogged in the direction Zeke had gone. Every few strides he leaped into the air for a better view. But trying to pick out a single person in that swirling mass of humanity was like trying to find the proverbial needle in a haystack.

After five minutes, Fargo halted. It was a lost cause. He returned to the post, meeting Ivy and Benjamin halfway.

"What the devil was that all about?" were the first words out of the muleskinner's mouth.

Fargo explained, and saw Ivy's head bob.

"Where Zeke is, Tom is," she said anxiously. "But what can he hope to gain? Frank has the prize money. Surely Tom wouldn't be crazy enough to try and steal it now?"

Benjamin spat tobacco at a beetle scurrying by. "Any *hombre* who would abuse you has to be *loco*. There's no tellin' what that coyote will do, Missy. Maybe we should warn Stockwell."

"No," Fargo said.

They looked at him. Ivy grew thoughtful. "Why not? What do you know that we don't?"

Fargo did not reply right away. There was no doubt he could trust them, but he would rather keep his suspicions to himself. For the moment, at any rate. "Let's just say that some things didn't add up until I put two and two together, and let it go at that."

"Hmmmph!" Benjamin snorted. "That's a fine how-do-you-do. We're in the dark, and you're talkin' in riddles. I think you're hidin' something, son."

"When the time is ripe," Fargo said, and would say no more, although they badgered him until he entered the post proper. Niles Kendall was behind the counter, showing a swatch of calico fabric to an elderly female customer. After the woman made her purchase and left, Fargo walked over. "I need to know a few things about tomorrow."

"Such as?"

"Where will you be?"

Kendall turned to a shelf and began stacking cans. "At the finish line, where I always am. Usually I'm the official judge, but Stockwell is this year. He practically begged me to be there, though. Claimed I could help if there's a dispute over the rules or the winner. And he's right. The Indians trust me."

"Who will handle things here while you're gone?"

"I close the store down until after the race. This place is so dead, it doesn't pay to keep it open." Kendall stopped stacking. "Why?"

"Just wondered," Fargo said. He had it all figured out now, except for one or two minor points. "When will the prize money be given out?"

"Right after the race. Stockwell insisted on presenting it himself. Which is only fair, I suppose. His paper did put the money up." The trader swiped at some dust. "We're leaving right after I give the signal for the race to start. Care to join us?"

"I'll be with the runners," Fargo said.

Kendall leaned on the counter. "I have to admit. When that peacock first waltzed in here and tried to sell me on the idea, I was leery. I foresaw all kinds of trouble. But it's worked out pretty well, if we don't count Scadding and that fellow you had to kill." He shook his head. "With all the gamblers and other riffraff that showed up, it's downright amazing."

"It's almost as if someone were keeping them in line," Fargo mentioned.

The trader did not hear. He had gone to deal with another customer. Since Fargo had a purchase of his own to make, he searched until he found the right aisle and measured out fifty feet of rope. It was probably twice as much as he needed, but he would rather have too much than too little. Afterward, he hunted up Benjamin. The muleskinner listened attentively, often chuckling and smacking his thigh.

"I got to hand it to you, young feller!" Benjamin remarked when Fargo was done. "You're a ring-tailed snorter, if ever there was one! I can't wait to see the looks on their faces!"

"Just be careful. Ivy would be crushed if anything happened to you."

Benjamin straightened. "I don't know whether to be glad that you think so highly of her, or mad that you think so poorly of me. I was holdin' my own against Comanches and the like when you were still suckin' on your ma's tit. So don't be lecturin' me. I'll be fine."

His plans set, Fargo had little to do until morning. Along with Ivy and those who were taking part in the race, he watched the long procession of spectators leave later that afternoon. A thick cloud of dust rose above the scores and scores of clattering wagons and countless riders. It was a festive occasion, with a lot of whooping and laughing and discharging of guns. By midnight they would be in position near the finish line.

Fargo estimated that close to a thousand people would be on hand for the end of the race. They had come from far and wide, from Taos and Santa Fe and Kansas City and points east. The Great Footrace promised to be one of the biggest events in the history of New Mexico Territory.

Once the sun set, the trading post was unnaturally quiet. Gone were the crowds. Gone were most of the tents. The lean-tos had been dismantled and used for firewood. Hardly a sound came from the four Indian encampments. The runners had retired early so they would be fresh and alert come race time.

The fragrance of perfume enveloped Fargo like a cloud. Ivy materialized at his side. A completely new Ivy. She had bought a low-cut dress that clung to her as if it were a second skin, highlighting her charms. The swell of her twin mounds reminded Fargo of melons about to burst. When she stepped around in front of him, the dress swished enticingly across her thighs. Her hair had been washed and combed to a fine sheen, framing her face in golden luster.

"What do you think, Skye?"

Fargo did not have to think. His aroused manhood was testimony to her beauty and sensual allure. "Show up in Santa Fe or Denver looking like that, and you can take your pick of any man you want."

Beaming, Ivy rotated on her toes. The hem swirled, showing a flash of milky thigh. "Mr. Kendall picked it out for me. Said it's all the rage back in the East." She leaned closer, imps dancing in her eyes. "Care to take a girl for a stroll?"

Fargo groaned. He would like nothing better, but he had to stay near the trading post until Benjamin relieved him about two in the morning. It was highly unlikely Stockwell would make his move before the race began, but Fargo was not leaving anything to chance.

"What's wrong?" Ivy asked.

"I can't," Fargo said, and wanted to kick himself when she stepped back and seemed to shrink into herself, hurt replacing the happiness.

"Why not?" Her voice was whispery sandpaper. "Have I done something wrong? Are you mad at me?"

"It's nothing like that," Fargo assured her and lightly gripped her shoulders. "Believe me. If I could, I'd whisk you into the woods so fast, it would make your head spin."

Ivy's lower lip quivered. "Then why? I mean, I know you're not the marrying kind, and all. But I didn't take you for one of those polecats who likes to kiss a gal just once, then move on to new conquests."

"You've got it all wrong—" Fargo began, but he was wasting his breath. Ivy tore from his grasp and dashed into the post, her long dress flying, her head bowed. He started to go after her, but stopped. She would understand once the whole mess was over with. Still, it bothered him. For all her newfound confidence, Ivy was as fragile as an egg. The scars she bore inside would take a long, long time to heal. He was not helping matters by confusing the hell out of her.

Irritated, Fargo retreated into the shadows and did not stir until Benjamin showed up. By then the fires in the Indian camps had died out and the lights in the trading post had been extinguished.

Stockwell and Kendall were two of the last to turn in. They sat on the porch for hours, drinking. Kendall rose first, stretched, and lumbered indoors.

From his hiding place, Fargo saw Stockwell rise. No one else was up and about. Stockwell walked a few yards, then gazed at the sky, extended his arms out from his sides, grinned, and chortled to himself.

"I've done it! This is the big one! In a week I'll be in

London! Then Paris, Rome, Athens! Ahhhh, life is sweet!" Stockwell danced a little jig. Staring at the store, he uttered a sinister laugh. "They're all sheep!" he declared. "And sheep were meant to be sheared!"

Doing his jig, Stockwell moved toward the sleeping quarters Kendall had provided for him. He cackled every few steps, putting a hand over his mouth so as not to awaken anyone.

Fargo never betrayed his presence. The time would come, soon enough. Everything must be just right. There must be no doubt in anyone's mind. Even the governor would be satisfied that Frank Stockwell was as guilty as sin.

Two hours later, Benjamin came. "What the hell did you do to Ivy?" the muleskinner promptly demanded. "The poor gal cried herself to sleep on my shoulder. She wouldn't tell me what had her so upset, but I gathered that you had something to do with it."

"I'll make it up to her," Fargo promised. "Here's the rope I bought." He handed it over. "Stockwell is in his room. Don't let him out of your sight once the race begins."

"There you go again," Benjamin rumbled. "Treatin' me like I'm a blamed five-year-old. We already done talked this out. I'll stick to that galoot like glue."

"Without being seen," Fargo reminded him.

Benjamin's jaw worked from side to side. "If I was ten years younger, I'd wallop you and take my lumps. Maybe you ought to have a sawbones check your ears. You don't hear so good."

Niles Kendall had put Fargo up in a small room at the back of the store. It was little more than a closet, but it was dry and warm and Fargo slept soundly. His internal clock woke him up before first light, and he was dressed and outside before anyone else.

Before any of the whites, that is. The Apaches, Navajos,

Pimas, and Maricopas had started to gather while it was still dark. They congregated in front of the post in quiet ranks, the Pimas and Maricopas close to one another and some distance from their long-standing enemies, the Apaches and Navajos.

When Fargo opened the gate, all eyes swung toward him. In the forefront of the Apaches stood Ish-kay-nay, proud and straight as ever. Hers was the only truly friendly face in the throng, her smile hinting at more than friendship. Fargo nodded, then went to saddle the Ovaro and the dun. He was leading them from the stable when Ivy arrived, dressed in her usual clothes.

"Morning," she said.

"Is it me, or has it suddenly grown colder?" Fargo said. The humor was not appreciated. She snatched the dun's reins and stared straight ahead, refusing to even look at him.

"Stick close to me," Fargo directed. "We'll be leaving when the runners do."

Ivy scanned the compound. "Where's Benjamin? He wasn't in our room when I woke up. I assumed he was with you."

"He won't be coming with us."

"What?" Ivy spun. "Has something happened to him?"

"No. You'll see him soon enough. Trust me. That's all I can say."

"Trust *you*?" Ivy said, and resorted to language that would make a schoolmarm faint. "I reckon I don't have any choice. But any woman who trusts a man is just asking for trouble."

Events unfolded swiftly from then on.

The whites who were taking part in the race gathered in their own little group in front of the post. They eyed the Indians with mutual distrust.

The men selected by Niles Kendall to take up posts along the Pecos were soon under way, each taking a flag that would be posted as a marker.

Presently, the trader climbed onto a stump. Fluent in the Navajo and Apache tongues, he gave a short speech in each before saying in English, "All of you know the rules. Runners may not hamper other runners. That means no pushing or shoving or tripping. Anyone who does so will be thrown out of the race. No taking shortcuts, or sneaking a bite of food or a drink. That applies to the river. Drink from it and you're out." He surveyed the crowd. "Any questions?"

None were posed. Fargo climbed onto the Ovaro to study the huge semicircle of participants. The ones he hoped to spot were not present.

Frank Stockwell stood near Kendall, smiling smugly. He tugged on the trader's sleeve and whispered something. Kendall frowned, then declared, "Before we get this shindig started, the man who organized the race has a few words to say."

They exchanged places. Stockwell introduced himself and launched into a long-winded tale about how hard he had worked to make the Great Footrace come about. The Indians were soon bored, and it was not long before the whites were fidgeting and muttering. Stockwell talked on until Kendall gave him a sharp poke.

"What? Oh." Stockwell puffed his chest out and waved cheerily. "Well, I guess that's all I have to say. Run a good race. Play fair. And may the best person win."

"Line up!" Kendall bawled.

There was an orderly rush to the starting line. Those who got there first did not have much of an advantage. So many people were pressed in close behind them that it would be next to impossible for anyone to gain much of a lead.

Niles Kendall drew his revolver, angled it at the clouds, and cocked the trigger. "Get set," he hollered.

The runners were as eager as greyhounds to be off. Bodies tensed, they bent forward, some balancing on their hands, many digging their feet into the ground. Most of the one hundred or so Apaches wore only breechcloths. An equal number of Navajos, and the seventy or eighty Pimas and Maricopas, had also stripped down. A majority of the whites were fully clothed, some even being so foolish as to wear heavy shirts and boots.

Ish-kay-nay was at the front. She wore the same short dress Fargo had seen on her the day before. Lithe form coiled, nostrils dilated, she concentrated on the terrain ahead—and nothing else.

At the crack of Kendall's pistol, the runners were off like a shot. The Indians ran in somber silence, but a lot of the whites whooped and yelled, losing breath and ground to those who did not.

Fargo watched until the rippling wave of flying limbs surged around a bend to the south. The last he saw, Ish-kay-nay was still in the forefront and running smoothly. "Let's go," he said to Ivy, spurring the stallion into a trot. As soon as they overtook the stragglers, he slowed.

"Shouldn't we be up in front of everyone?" the blonde asked. "How do you expect to keep track of them from way back here?"

"The men posted along the river will keep a lid on things," Fargo said. "We have something more important to do."

"Mind confiding what that is?"

"Be patient."   •

Ivy hissed and made an unflattering comment about his intelligence. "No doubt about it, Skye Fargo. You are the most aggravating man I have ever met, and that takes some doing."

Fargo shifted frequently to study the trail behind them. He did not have long to wait. Soon Niles Kendall came galloping along, alone. The trader slowed when Fargo held a hand aloft. "Where's Stockwell?"

Kendall did not stop. "We hadn't gone a hundred yards

and his damn horse started limping," he called out as he flew on past. "He told me to go on ahead. Said he'll catch up as soon as he can. Just our luck! Be seeing you."

Fargo drew rein. Ivy did the same, more confused than ever.

"What is it now?"

"We're going back."

She started to quiz him, but Fargo did not listen. Slanting into the woods, he bore to the east, swinging in a loop that brought them up on the rear of the trading post through thick cover. He had the Henry out and a cartridge in the chamber before the high walls loomed through the trees.

Ivy did not pester him again. When he climbed down and tied the pinto to a cottonwood, she followed suit with the dun. When he crept to the southeast corner and crouched, she dogged his footsteps.

No sounds could be heard within the palisade. Fargo glided along the wall, avoiding dry twigs. Near the southwest corner, he slowed. From within rose the nicker of a horse and muffled voices. Warily, he took a look. No one was in front of the palisade. The gates were wide open. Taking a gamble, he dashed to the nearest and hunkered in its shadow.

"Come on, damn it! We don't have all day!"

The voice was Frank Stockwell's. Fargo edged forward far enough to glimpse the compound. A wagon was parked near the front door, its tail down. The door hung by one hinge, partially shattered. Standing on the porch was Stockwell, and he was not alone. Tom Grifter, Boothe, Pardee, and two other hardcases who had been in the ravine the other night were there. Judging by the noises wafting through the door, the rest were inside.

Fingernails bit into Fargo's arm. Ivy's lips touched his ear. "Tom and Frank! They were working together all along! And you knew it!"

"I had a hunch," Fargo whispered. But it was more than that. Grifter had mentioned having a boss. A boss who just happened to know *exactly* when Ivy would leave Taos and *exactly* which route she would take. Information that only one other person besides Ivy had known. He wondered if Stockwell had ever learned that Grifter tried to steal the prize money for himself.

"But how did—" Ivy began, falling silent when figures appeared in the doorway. In the lead was Zeke. He backed out, kicked the door aside, and motioned. Other cutthroats were framed in the opening, straining to slide a large safe on rollers.

"They're stealing Kendall's life savings!" Ivy whispered.

The trader had brought it on himself by bragging about his hoard. Fargo did not know how much was in there, but it was probably a lot. Ten thousand dollars would be a fair guess. Add to that the seven thousand in prize money and Stockwell's cut of the money earned by the gamblers and whiskey peddlers, and it was a safe bet that Frank Stockwell stood to be twenty to twenty-five thousand dollars richer by the end of the day.

"We must stop them," Ivy said. Rashly, she tried to go past him.

Fargo clasped her wrist. "Not quite yet." The horses belonging to the outlaw band were tied to the hitching post north of the store, close to the stable. He looked, but at that distance he could not tell whether Benjamin had done what he asked.

"Help out! All of you!" Frank Stockwell commanded.

Even with eight men handling the safe, rolling it down the steps and over to the wagon was a monumental task. It distracted them, allowing Fargo to reach a water trough just inside and to the right. Ivy stayed at the gate.

Sweating and swearing, the outlaws hoisted the safe off the ground. They almost had it level with the wagon bed when Fargo rose above the trough. Leveling the Henry, he shouted, "That's as far as you go, boys! Set it down and drop your hardware!"

Boothe, Pardee, and several others let go and spun, stabbing for their six-shooters. Those left holding the safe were unable to bear the weight. Automatically, they scattered, but one of them was not quick enough. An unholy shriek tore from his throat as the safe smashed onto his right leg, crushing it and pinning him flat.

Fargo squeezed off a shot a split second ahead of Boothe. The gunman staggered backward, into the porch, a red dot where his left pupil had been. Others fired. Fargo had to duck as lead drilled through the trough above him and on both sides.

Ivy's rifle boomed. Some of the gunmen turned their attention to her. One keeled over. Stockwell was yelling but he could not be heard above the din.

Fargo heaved up and snapped off a shot that toppled another member of the gang. Pardee and four others were flying toward their horses, firing on the run, a steady hailstorm of slugs that forced Ivy to jerk back and Fargo to fall flat near the end of the trough.

The Trailsman saw Pardee reach his mount. Vaulting into the saddle, Pardee hauled on the reins and slapped his legs against its side. The horse did not move. Stupefied, he did it again, with the same result. Bending, he discovered why. All their mounts had been hobbled by short lengths of rope.

Suddenly a new element was added. A rifle poked from the small door on the stable loft. Two swift shots sent Pardee crashing from the saddle. Benjamin's version of a Comanche war whoop rang out.

Over half the gunmen were dead or dying. Those who were left, caught in the open, flung their guns to the dirt and thrust their hands high. Zeke was among them, but not

Frank Stockwell and Tom Grifter. Realizing they could not make it across the compound, they backpedaled into the trading post, Grifter firing wildly.

Fargo sprang up and leaped over the trough. Zigzagging, he ran to the building. Hesitating just long enough to verify that the muleskinner had the other outlaws covered, he scrambled onto the planks and rolled. Hot lead shattered a window above him, the slugs tearing into the spot he had just vacated.

Flat on his back, Fargo answered with two shots of his own. Whoever had been firing at him stopped. Instantly, he snaked to the door and rose on his right knee. Somewhere inside a table crashed over. Setting the Henry at his feet, he drew the Colt and removed his hat.

"You'll never get us, Trailsman! Do you hear me?"

That was Tom Grifter, panicking. Fargo hurled his hat through the doorway, whirled, and threw himself at the window. Thunder rocked his ears as he cleared the bottom sill with inches to spare. Muzzle flashes gave him targets. He fired at the nearest as he dropped, then rolled as the floor next to his face was chewed up.

A table and chairs offered a haven. Fargo pushed up and saw a dark silhouette over by the bar. A derringer cracked thinly. His trigger finger pumped twice, and at the last shot, Frank Stockwell tottered into the open, the smoking derringer hanging useless at his side. Stockwell's knees buckled and he pitched onto them.

Fargo took aim. But another shot was not needed. The man who had connived and hoodwinked everyone from the governor on down had told his last lie. Frank Stockwell thudded onto his face and was still.

"I've got you, bastard!"

For a few seconds, Fargo had forgotten about Tom Grifter. He pivoted, knowing he was too late even before he saw Grifter behind an overturned table, a cocked revolver pointed at his chest. Grifter was smirking.

Just then someone rushed through the doorway. It was Ivy Cambridge. She fired a fraction of a second before Grifter, the lead punching him backward and throwing off his aim. The slug meant for Fargo plowed into the wall instead. Grifter shifted toward Ivy. She shot him as he raised his pistol, shot him as he stumbled, shot him a third time as he fell against the counter, and put her last shot into him as he sank to the floor.

For long moments the room was quiet. Finally, Ivy twirled the Smith & Wesson into her holster, glanced at Fargo, and grinned. "Lordy, that felt good."

By that evening, riders were racing to Fort Union, Santa Fe, and Taos with the news. No one was much interested in the story of the race itself. Fourteen runners were disqualified for sneaking drinks from the Pecos, two of them Pimas, another a Maricopa. Of the top twenty finishers, twelve were Apaches, seven were Navajos, and one was a young man from a mining community high in the mountains.

Fargo was not the least bit surprised to learn that a nubile Mescalero maiden of his acquaintance had won, handily. As the sun sank to the west, he leaned against a porch post and smiled. He could relax, enjoy himself, get drunk if he wanted. He deserved to celebrate, after all he had been through. It was over at last.

Or was it?

Ivy appeared near the stable. She had on the new dress she'd bought, and she gestured for him to join her. He moved to the steps, then froze. Ish-kay-nay was at the gate, wearing her finest buckskin, a red ribbon in her hair, and a seductive smile. She beckoned.

The Trailsman looked from one to the other. "Damn!" he swore under his breath. What was a man to do?

LOOKING FORWARD!
The following is the opening
section from the next novel in the exciting
Trailsman series from Signet:

**THE TRAILSMAN #191
TARGET GOLD**

*1860, New Mexico, at the edge of the
Apache Forest in the shadow of
Alegros Mountain, the beginning of a
twisted trail of betrayal and deceit . . .*

It was a day designed for making mistakes, for violating
rules and suspending caution, lazy, hot, indolent, with the
fragrance of purple prairie clover caressing the air. The big
man with the lake blue eyes rode the magnificent Ovaro
slowly, savoring the day. A long pond glistened in the sunlight as he moved the horse through a cluster of red cedars.
It was a day when the young woman lying naked on the
rock just back from the pond seemed entirely in place, as
though she simply belonged there. Skye Fargo pulled the
horse to a stop, peered through the trees. The young woman
seemed to be asleep and he saw her clothes, blouse, skirt,
half-slip, and bloomers, spread out on the rock beside her.
He nosed the horse closer down a narrow pathway, saw the
young woman sit up as she heard him and pull a leafy
branch to her to form a dubious screen.

He moved into sight at the end of the little path, almost

at the edge of the rock. "Thank heavens. Somebody to help me," the young woman said, keeping the leafy branch pulled in front of her. It didn't conceal terribly much and he glimpsed heavy breasts with large, deep red nipples and matching areolas, a body edging heaviness, waist, belly, legs, all well fleshed out. Yet she was young enough to carry everything, her skin smooth and tight. "My horse threw me into the water and ran off. He's grazing somewhere at the far end of the pond," she said. "Everything I had on was soaked through. I took my clothes off so they'd dry. My name's Millie Jones."

"Skye Fargo," the big man said, his lake blue eyes taking in a face that was pretty enough, round with even features and dark, curly hair with some hard lines around a wide mouth.

"Do you think you could get my horse for me, Fargo?" the young woman asked. "I'd really be grateful. I'd have to wait for my clothes to dry and then I might never catch him. I borrowed him."

"I'll give it a try," he said and rode past the rock. She continued to hold the tree branch pulled to her and he decided it might embarrass her if he told her how little it concealed. He passed the edge of the rock, rode slowly to the water's edge, followed the curve of the pond till he saw the horse, a stubby brown gelding foraging in a patch of sweetclover. He moved slowly but saw that the horse didn't even look up as he neared. He didn't seem at all skittish, Fargo noted. He reached the horse, took hold of the reins, and the gelding came along without any sign of resistance.

He led the horse back along the edge of the pond to the rock where Millie waited. She pulled the leafy branch to her again as he tied the gelding to a low branch. "Just thank you doesn't seem enough," the young woman said. "I could've been out here for hours and still had a long walk back. Do you mind if I let this branch go? It's hard to hold on to it."

"Be my guest," Fargo said.

"You look like a man who's seen plenty of girls without their clothes on," Millie said.

"A few." Fargo smiled as he swung from the saddle. The branch sprang into place as Millie released her hold on it and he had an unobstructed view of her. Her youth kept the heavy breasts from sagging and just below a very round belly with the hint of a crease, a bushy, untidy black nap covered a very round pubic mound.

"I know only one way to really thank a man, Fargo," Millie said and leaned back on her elbows, her full thighs parting ever so slightly. She radiated a simple, unvarnished sexuality, he realized, no coy pretenses to her.

"You offering?" he asked mildly.

"Let's say I'd enjoy saying thank you," she said and the heavy breasts swayed as she shifted position.

"What were you doing out here?" Fargo asked.

"Had a day off and went for a ride," Millie said.

"Where'd you come from?"

"Stockwell," she said and he nodded. It was one of those towns that existed for passing trailhands and prospectors, the kind of town where no one ever thought about putting down roots. He decided to voice the question that came to his mind.

"You a saloon girl?" Fargo asked.

She gave a slow, almost sheepish smile. "That make a difference?"

"Guess not," he said, lowering himself to the rock beside her.

"Then let's stop talking and enjoy ourselves," Millie said and her hands began to unbutton his shirt. He unstrapped his gunbelt and let it slide to the ground. There was every reason to accept her suggestion. He had the time and she was certainly creating the inclination. He was due in Willow Flats but he was almost a week early. Besides, it was a day for enjoying, a day designed for dalliance. His shirt came off and he brought his hard-muscled torso over her, touched her breasts, which gave way with pillowy softness. He shed his trousers and her round belly was another mound of softness and he felt her thighs come open at once and lift to come against his hips. "Yes. Jesus, yes," Millie gasped as his lips closed around one deep breast, drawing its pillowy softness into his mouth. The flat rock was warm but unyielding and he closed both arms around her, pulling her with him to a dark green bed of nut moss.

He had just pulled her down to the moss when the two shots exploded. The first sent a little spray of rock chips into the air just over his head. The second hurtled past his shoulder. Both would have gone into his back if he hadn't pulled Millie from the rock a split second earlier. Her cry mingled with the sound of another shot that hit the ground as Fargo rolled from her. "Goddamn sons of bitches," she screamed, both anger and fright in her voice. But Fargo was rolling, reaching out to scoop up his gunbelt as he flung himself into the thicket of trees behind the rock.

Inside the trees, he turned, strapped on his gunbelt, and drew the big Colt. Two more shots exploded and thudded into the trees, grazing Millie's full rear as she scrambled frantically along the ground toward the trees. When she was close enough, he reached out, grabbed her hand, and pulled her into the trees with him. Her back to him, she pushed to her knees. "I didn't know . . ." she began. He cut her off as he put one foot against her ample rear and pushed hard. She fell forward into the trees with a yelp.

"No more damn lies," he hissed from one knee, peering through the trees to the thicket of red cedar beyond the rock. She said nothing as she stayed low and crawled to him, her silence admission. "How many are there?" Fargo asked.

"Four," she whispered. He risked a glance over the top of the rock and two more shots came instantly. They were in the cedars directly across from him, but he needed a better bead on them. He kept his eyes on the cedars as he spoke to Millie.

"The land behind us goes up in a thick tree cover. You start running. Don't try to be quiet, just stay low. Keep running till you reach the top of the rise," Fargo said. "Remember, stay low."

"Where are you going to be?" Millie asked.

"Looking out for you," he said. Despite the vulnerability of her position and her nakedness, Millie fixed a skeptical frown on him. "Do it, now," Fargo hissed. "You're out of bargaining time." She turned, crouched, and started to run through the trees, almost instantly moving upward along the hillside. Fargo's eyes fixed on the cedars beyond the rock, the Colt raised. The movement in the trees was quick, a volley of shots erupting as the gunmen fired. Fargo spotted the two places where the shots resounded, made a split-second calculation from the movement of the trees and the staccato echo of the gunfire. The gunmen were in pairs, a few feet from each other.

He measured distance, allowed for movement, and fired off four quick shots. Three groans of pain followed his shots, gasped cries that were followed by the sound of bodies falling. A fourth voice cursed and Fargo heard, then saw, the flurry of movement in the trees as the figure turned and ran. Following in a loping crouch, Fargo glimpsed the figure a dozen yards from him, racing through the thicket. Making no attempt to be quiet, Fargo bulled his way forward and saw the man stop and spin, gun in hand. The man took a moment to squint through the trees and find his target before he brought his gun up. It was a fatal moment as Fargo's Colt exploded, a single shot directly on target. The man arched backward as though he were suddenly yanked by an invisible rope. He crashed into a tree, stayed there a moment before sliding downward to the ground, his chest a spreading red stain. Fargo straightened, listened, and heard only silence. Millie had reached the top of the hill.

"Come on down. It's over," he called and moved to the lifeless figure against the tree as he heard Millie coming downhill. He stepped to where the other three figures were near each other a few yards away, all silent, beyond answering questions. He undid his gunbelt, returned to the rock, and pulled on his trousers and shirt as Millie appeared. Despite her nakedness, she managed a defensive glower in her round face. "Start talking," Fargo growled. "No bullshit, honey. You knew they were waiting."

She blinked. "I didn't know they were going to shoot you," Millie said. "Honest, I didn't. They said they were old friends of yours who wanted to play a joke on you. They said there were two places you'd be likely to come through on your way to Willow Flats. This was one of them." Fargo felt the furrow dig into his brow at Millie's words. They were right and what happened had been no chance dry-gulching. It had been planned. "They sent me here, told me what to do and what to say," Millie went on. "They sent Lily to the other place."

"The road by the Blackjack Oak alongside Shad Creek?" He frowned and Millie nodded. "Who's Lily?" he asked.

"She works with me at the saloon," Millie said.

"Then the others are waiting there with her. She's lying around naked, too, I take it," Fargo said.

Millie nodded. "They told us both the same thing when they hired us. They never said anything about shooting, honest they didn't."

Fargo didn't disbelieve her. She had been as surprised as he when the shots erupted. Perhaps angrier. "Put your clothes on. I'm going to visit your friend Lily. Only I'm going to do the surprising, this time," he said. He strode to the Ovaro and waited in the saddle as Millie hurriedly pulled on clothes and climbed onto her horse. She stayed close behind him as he led the way north through a pass between high rock, into a line of shadbush, his eyes narrowed in thought. Somebody knew he was on his way to Willow Flats and wanted to make sure he didn't get there. Why? The question danced inside his head. That somebody knew more about why he was going to Willow Flats than he did, Fargo muttered inwardly. He'd been hired to break trail but that's all he knew. It seemed there was a lot more.

Fargo put aside the questions that tumbled inside him as the line of Blackjack Oak appeared, the small creek threading its way beside the thick, scaly, black-bark trees. It was indeed one of the two routes most folks would take on their way east to Willow Flats, Fargo mused as his eyes swept the trees and the creek. When he reached the midway point, he crossed over the creek and went into the trees, halted, and swung to the ground. "You, too," he muttered to Millie, who obeyed quickly. With a blouse and skirt on, she looked terribly ordinary, he observed. "Stay here till I get back," he ordered. "Don't make things worse for yourself."

"I'm not moving," Millie said and Fargo led the Ovaro on through the trees. The creek burbled a dozen yards away, moving in and out of sunlight, and after another hundred yards Fargo tethered the horse to a branch and went on alone. He moved slowly, on silent, pantherlike steps, his eyes flicking back and forth inside the trees and to the creek when he suddenly halted, dropping to one knee. He peered at the clear patch of ground alongside the creek where the young woman lay naked, stretched out with arms over her head, her clothes hung on a nearby branch. But this time Fargo pulled his eyes from her, turning his attention to the trees. He peered into the oak, his gaze moving carefully, slowly, finally halting as the figures took shape.

Three men, he counted, scanned the trees beyond them until he concluded they were the only three. Their eyes were focused beside the creek, where the young woman lay naked. She hadn't Millie's overblown figure, Fargo noted, her body smaller, thinner. Yet she eminently qualified as a lure. Fargo unholstered the Colt and moved another dozen silent steps closer until there were no major branch clusters in his way. The three figures were clear in his sights, though their faces were turned away from him.

"This surprise party is over," Fargo said. The three figures stiffened and then spun toward him. "Freeze and nobody gets hurt," Fargo warned.

They weren't deaf but they certainly were dumb, Fargo concluded as the three went for their guns. "Get him," one snarled. Fargo fired, four shots perfectly placed, firing so fast they sounded almost as one. The three figures fell in three different directions, as if in a strange parody of a flower unfolding its petals. The moment was so brief it almost seemed not to have happened, but it had, and the three figures lay still on the ground. Fargo glanced at the girl by the creek, saw her sitting up, immobile, clutching a blouse to herself.

"Stay there," he ordered, lifting his voice and shouting back into the trees. "Millie, get your ass over here. Bring your horse," he called, holstered the Colt, and heard her pushing her way through the trees. "Go down and wait with her," he ordered as Millie came into sight. As Millie went to join Lily, Fargo walked to the three figures and halted, stepping from one to the other. The frown dug into his brow as he peered at the third one. "I'll be damned," he muttered, finally turning and going back to retrieve the Ovaro. The frown was still digging into his brow as he went to the creek. Lily had her clothes on and waited beside Millie and he swept both girls with a hard glance. "The one with the scar on his chin hire you?" Fargo questioned and both young women nodded. "What else did he have to say?" Fargo asked.

"Just what I told you. Nothing more," Millie answered as Lily nodded vigorously.

"His name's Willie Stratton. He's a holdup man, operates mostly out of Oklahoma and Kansas, prefers stagecoaches. He spent five years behind bars because of me," Fargo said. "Attacked the wrong coach at the wrong time."

"Is that why he did this, to get back at you?" Millie asked.

Fargo turned the question over in his mind for a moment before crinkling up his face as he shook his head. "Can't see that. Willie Stratton's a small-time shit. Revenge wouldn't be his thing. It just wouldn't fit him," Fargo said, thinking aloud. Yet Willie had gone to great lengths to devise an elaborate dry-gulch. He had to have a special reason, Fargo thought. And there was the other thing that didn't fit. How did Willie Stratton know he was on his way to Willow Flats? And why did he know it? Fargo's eyes went to the two young women. "You sure he didn't say anything else? Think, damn it," Fargo barked.

"Nothing else, only what he ordered us to do," Millie said.

"He told us it was going to be a joke on you," Lily said.

"Isn't that just what I said?" Millie put in. He paused, deciding they were too scared for anything but the truth.

"Go home, and keep quiet about this," Fargo said.

"I'm not saying a word," Millie said.

"Me neither," Lily echoed.

"Get out of here," Fargo growled and the two young women climbed onto their horses and hurried away. He let them disappear from sight before he rode on. He turned from the stand of blackjack oak and rode south as the day began to slide into dusk. He stayed south and bedded down in a cluster of red ash as night fell, slowly munching a cold strip of beef jerky. He had decided to stay away from Stockwell. There was no reason for him to visit the town. The attempt on his life had failed. It was over, finished. He'd pursue the questions that stayed when he reached Willow Flats. But sleep refused to offer its comforts so quickly and he found himself lying awake, the attack still prodding him.

Yesterdays swam out of his memory. It had been a long time since he had ended Willie Stratton's attack on the stagecoach that ended with Willie going to jail. Willie had been out of jail at least five years since then. Why would he suddenly decide to strike back? Fargo grimaced at the question. It just didn't fit. Something else had brought Willie Stratton to plot his fancy dry-gulching. Fargo's thoughts went to the man who had hired him by mail with an advance too sweet to turn down. Fargo knew him only by his name on the letter, Ben Bartley. The letter had given him a place and a date and the need for his talents. The letter had given no hint of anything else. Fargo swore softly, turned on his side, and forced himself to keep his eyes closed, letting only the distant howl of red wolves intrude on his thoughts until sleep finally came to him.

He woke with the morning sun, washed at a tiny stream, and breakfasted on prickly pear. He rode southeast, used the tall peak of the Alegros Mountain at his left as a guide. The rutted antelope trail he followed was the most direct route to the Sandy and Cactus rivers. The two rivers, flowing some thousand yards apart, ran a parallel course that would eventually lead to Willow Flats, which sat between both. The Sandy and the Cactus were both slow, shallow waterways, hardly the Mississippi and the Missouri. Yet their location in the arid New Mexico landscape let Willow Flats prosper as a place that could be reached by wagon and small riverboats.

But Willow Flats was still two days away and Fargo refused to hurry. There'd be plenty of time to satisfy questions. Curiosity could take a back seat to relaxation, he decided. The day was a copy of the one before, pleasant and lazy, made for enjoying the lush trail as it wound its way through clusters of smooth sumac and live oak. It almost made one forget how arid and harsh this land could be and that the Apache and Mescalero were always there, an ever-present, savage shadow. The Apache, the Mescalero, they knew the land, better than anyone knew it, how to hunt on it, fight on it, how to use its harshness, how to live with it. They plundered, conquered, and killed the Zuni, Hopi, and Pima with the same merciless efficiency they did the white man, perhaps with greater enjoyment, because the tribes hadn't the numbers or the weapons the white man possessed.

But Fargo saw no signs of Apache on the antelope trail, only the hoofprints of those who'd come this way, so many they outnumbered the signs of antelope. The day stayed warm and soft and he rode slowly. The sun moved into the afternoon sky when the trail widened and he saw a pond appear. He let the Ovaro move to the pond. Taking a quick glance at the water, he saw that it seemed fresh, a small stream feeding into it at the far end. But as the horse drank, Fargo's eyes narrowed at the hoofprints at the edge of the pond, a half dozen not more than a few hours old. His gaze followed the prints as they moved away from the pond. That was ordinary enough, he grunted silently, but his eyes narrowed further and he sent the Ovaro forward. The hoofprints didn't go down the trail. Instead, they turned into the thickness of the trees a dozen yards beyond the pond.

Fargo felt the skin on the back of his neck grow tight. He halted and let the wisdom of the trail speak to him. Any behavior or sign that parted from the normal, the ordinary, was a warning. Men that paused to water their horses would be expected to ride on along the trail. That would be the normal, the ordinary. But these had suddenly turned into the woods. Why, Fargo asked himself. To lie in wait? His lips pulled back in a grimace. It seemed ridiculous to think there'd be a second attempt to dry-gulch him. Yet he couldn't dismiss the thought and another kind of wisdom pulled at him, this told him by an old cowhand, Charley Hinton, years ago.

"Anybody can get kicked by a horse," Charley had said. "And you can get kicked by the same horse in another place or a different horse in the same place. But you should never get kicked by the same horse in the same place twice." Being dry-gulched two days in a row was to be kicked by the same horse in the same place twice, Fargo muttered to himself. He wasn't about to let that happen. Moving the Ovaro forward at a walk, he slipped the Colt from its holster and held it against his leg where it wouldn't be seen but would let him fire at least five seconds faster. As he moved closer to where the hoofprints turned into the woods, he kept his head low but peered out from under the brim of his hat. He peered hard into the foliage as he reached the spot where the prints entered the woods and he felt the tiny beads of perspiration coating his brow.

Then he caught it, the tiny movement, branches being pushed aside. His hand with the Colt in it came up firing as he kicked heels into the Ovaro's ribs and the horse bolted forward. Fargo heard the results of his shots in the groans of pain and the sound of falling bodies as he flattened himself in the saddle. A hail of answering shots came, but the Ovaro had charged past the spot and the bullets fell short of their target. Fargo vaulted from the saddle, yanking the rifle from its saddlecase as he did, and landing at the edge of the trail. He dove into the trees, spun, and dropped to one knee, the big Henry raised in both hands. The three horsemen charged out of the woods at the other side of the trail, spraying bullets, depending on volume rather than accuracy. Fargo stayed down, letting the hail of bullets whistle past him, over him, and slam into trees on both sides of him. When he put the rifle to his shoulder, his first shot hit the nearest horseman and he saw the man topple backward over the rump of his horse. The other two attackers started to veer away but the rifle cracked again two shots, and both figures stiffened before they fell from their horses to land almost atop one another.

Fargo waited, not moving, his eyes on the woods, his ears straining for the faintest sound. But he heard nothing, not the brush of a leaf, not the pull of a branch, not a groan or harsh breath. But he continued to wait until, satisfied, he straightened up. It was over but it had been another ambush aimed at him. There was no doubt in his mind about that any longer and he frowned as he walked to the three figures, realizing that he was more confounded than angry. He reached the first figure lying facedown and turned the man onto his back. "Goddamn," he heard himself mutter as he stared down at the man. "Mickey Mulvaney." Once more the past rose up to prod at him, memories and images he'd all but forgotten about. Mickey Mulvaney was another holdup artist. He preferred banks, Fargo remembered.

He'd never sent Mickey Mulvaney to jail, Fargo recalled, but he had wrecked his plans more than once. The frown dug deeper into Fargo's brow. First Willie Stratton and now Mickey Mulvaney, both out to dry-gulch him. Why all of a sudden, Fargo pondered. Only one thing seemed certain. The attacks were no echoes out of the past, sudden attempts at vengeance. There was something more. Both had picked spots he was likely to find on his way to Willow Flats. Both had clearly known he was going there. But how? And why were they each so anxious to stop him? He swore softy in frustration as he bent down and began to go through Mickey Mulvaney's pockets. The first turned out cigarette paper, the second loose change. When he fished into an inside jacket pocket he drew out a folded circular, opened it up, and felt the wave of astonishment sweep over him.

NOTICE!

GOLD SHIPMENT TO LEAVE WILLOW FLATS ON

OR ABOUT JULY 10, 1860

Mr. Skye Fargo, the Trailsman, will take the shipment through. Space is still available. Anyone with gold to ship must make arrangements with the Willow Flats Trading Bank by July 1.

A. Baldwin, Sheriff

"This has got to be the stupidest goddamn thing I've ever seen," Fargo said as astonishment turned to anger.

LEGENDS OF THE WEST

☐ **SCARLET PLUME by Frederick Manfred.** Amid the bloody 1862 Sioux uprising, a passion that crosses all boundaries is ignited. Judith Raveling is a white woman captured by the Sioux Indians. Scarlet Plume, nephew of the chief who has taken Judith for a wife, is determined to save her. But surrounded by unrelenting brutal fighting and vile atrocities, can they find a haven for a love neither Indian nor white woman would sanction? (184238—$4.50)

☐ **WHITE APACHE by Frank Burleson.** Once his name was Nathanial Barrington, one of the finest officers in the United States Army. Now his visions guide him and his new tribe on daring raids against his former countrymen. Amid the smoke of battle and in desire's fiercest blaze, he must choose between the two proud peoples who fight for his loyalty and the two impassioned women who vie for his soul. (187296—$5.99)

☐ **WHISPERS OF THE MOUNTAIN by Tom Hron.** White men had come to Denali, the great sacred mountain looming over the Indians' ancestral land in Alaska, searching for gold that legend said lay hidden on its heights. A shaman died at the hands of a greed-mad murderer—his wife fell captive to the same human monster. Now in the deadly depth of winter, a new hunt began on the treacherous slopes of Denali—not for gold but for the most dangerous game of all. (187946—$5.99)

☐ **WHISPERS OF THE RIVER by Tom Hron.** Passion and courage, greed and daring—a stirring saga of the Alaskan gold rush. With this rush of brawling, lusting, striving humanity, walked Eli Bonnet, a legendary lawman who dealt out justice with his gun . . . and Hannah Twigg, a woman who dared death for love and everything for freedom. (187806—$5.99)

*Prices slightly higher in Canada

Buy them at your local bookstore or use this convenient coupon for ordering.

PENGUIN USA
P.O. Box 999 — Dept. #17109
Bergenfield, New Jersey 07621

Please send me the books I have checked above.
I am enclosing $_____ (please add $2.00 to cover postage and handling). Send check or money order (no cash or C.O.D.'s) or charge by Mastercard or VISA (with a $15.00 minimum). Prices and numbers are subject to change without notice.

Card #_____ Exp. Date _____
Signature_____
Name_____
Address_____
City _____ State _____ Zip Code _____

For faster service when ordering by credit card call **1-800-253-6476**

Allow a minimum of 4-6 weeks for delivery. This offer is subject to change without notice.